"My lord, I know what my heart is feeling."

"What is your heart feeling, my lady?"

"Strangely elated. As though on the verge of some new and wonderful discovery." She traced the outline of his mouth with her finger.

His eyes were narrowed on her with such intensity, she felt a quick twist of fear.

"Do you know what happens when you tempt a sleeping wolf, my lady?"

When she said nothing, he whispered, "You become its prey. The wolf, once awakened, devours you."

He released her hand and turned away. His snub was like a knife to her heart.

Over his shoulder he said softly, "Go now and rest for the morrow's journey."

Kylia felt tears spring to her eyes and brushed them away with the back of her hand. She would not permit herself to weep over this man. Nor any man…!

* * *

The Betrayal
Harlequin Historical #666—July 2003

THE BETRAYAL

RUTH LANGAN

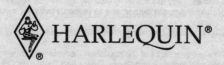

HARLEQUIN®

TORONTO • NEW YORK • LONDON
AMSTERDAM • PARIS • SYDNEY • HAMBURG
STOCKHOLM • ATHENS • TOKYO • MILAN • MADRID
PRAGUE • WARSAW • BUDAPEST • AUCKLAND

ISBN 0-373-29266-X

THE BETRAYAL

Copyright © 2003 by Ruth Ryan Langan

Visit us at www.eHarlequin.com

Printed in U.S.A.

For Randi,
With her sweet nature and delightful wit.

And for Tom,
Who lives to tease.

Chapter One

Scottish Highlands, 1559

The clang of sword against shield rang in the Highland forest as barbarians rose up from their places of concealment to attack the horsemen in plaid who rode toward them in single file. Caught unawares, there was nowhere the Highland warriors could reassemble their forces. They had no choice but to put up a brave front, even though they were badly outnumbered.

"They knew we were coming, my lord." Finlay, the old man who had ridden with the clan MacCallum for more than two score years, caught the young lord's arm. "Ye must turn the men back. Else, all will be lost."

The thought of retreat went against everything Grant MacCallum believed in. But common sense had to rule over ego. These men had wives and families depending on them. If they were to stand and fight against such overwhelming odds, most would be lost, leaving their clan with even more widows and orphans grieving their losses.

Through gritted teeth he shouted the order. "Sound the call to retreat."

Minutes later the wail of the pipes had the horsemen turning and plunging into thickets to escape the swords of their enemy. Grant stood his ground, fighting alongside old Finlay until every last man had made good his escape. Then, watching the old man's back until he, too, was free, Grant pulled himself onto his steed and took off with a thunder of hoofbeats.

As he made his way back to his Highland fortress, he mulled this latest in a series of chilling events. Since he'd been declared laird of the MacCallums, they had twice been met by an army of invaders at the very spot they'd hoped to mount a surprise attack. Once could have been considered an accident. The second time could no longer be considered an isolated incident. Taken together, they proved without a doubt that he was being betrayed. But since plans of this march had been known to only a handful of his most trusted Council members, he now knew that the betrayal was personal, and was coming from one of his own.

"We just heard the news." Grant's brother Dougal, younger by thirteen months, was breathless from racing up the stairs of the fortress to his chambers. Though he was shorter and broader, his hair and eyes a paler version of Grant's, the two bore a striking resemblance to each other.

Behind him trailed a tall woman dressed like a cloistered nun, wearing a black gown and head cover, with a veil covering her face. She crossed the room, quiet and stiff backed, and settled herself into a chair set before the fire.

"Aunt Hazlet." Grant turned from the balcony, where he'd been deep in thought, and crossed to the woman to press his hand to hers. It was the only sign of affection she permitted.

She folded her hands in her lap. Even her

voice had the clipped, precise tone of a mother superior. "I've been told by the Council that you didn't catch the invaders, nephew. You realize the people will now think you a coward for running from a fight."

Grant turned toward the flames of the fire. "What others think of me is the least of my worries."

"What can be worse than letting invaders go free, or having your own people brand you a coward?"

"What's worse? I'll tell you. Betrayal." Grant spat the word.

"What are you saying?" Dougal crossed the room to stand beside his brother.

Grant shot a glance at old Finlay, who stood quietly across the room. "Our attackers knew we were coming. They were hiding along the bend in the trail, where fighting would be the most difficult."

Dougal's eyes narrowed in thought. "Perhaps they saw the glint of your shields."

"There was no sunlight in the forest," the old man said softly.

"The sound of men's voices, then. Or the thundering of horses' hooves."

Grant shook his head. "I'd cautioned my warriors to remain silent. The horses were walking. I tell you, our enemies had been forewarned of our arrival."

Dougal shot him a look. "Are you saying there's a traitor in our midst?"

"Exactly." Grant picked up a length of plaid and tossed it over his shoulder before strapping on his scabbard.

Seeing it, his brother touched a hand to his arm. "Where are you going?"

"To the Mystical Kingdom."

That had Dougal shaking his head. "You jest." Seeing the flare of anger in his brother's eyes, he arched a brow. "Nay, I see that you're serious." He turned to their aunt to back him up. "But surely you know what they say about that place."

Grant nodded. "Aye. I've heard a lifetime of tales about the dragon that guards the loch, protecting the witches who live there. But if the legends be true, and a man successfully crosses into their kingdom, those witches can be forced to reveal their secrets to him."

"You're mad."

"Perhaps." Grant picked up his dirk and tucked it into his boot. "But the people of Duncrune have declared me laird of the clan MacCallum. With that privilege comes the responsibility of keeping those under my protection safe. If that means I must risk my life, so be it." He laid a hand on his brother's shoulder. "I'll not return to Duncrune Castle until I have what I seek."

"And what is that?"

"The truth."

Their aunt got to her feet. "You'd take the word of a witch as truth?"

"Am I better off trusting one who would betray me?"

"You don't know that to be true."

"I know it in my heart, Aunt." Grant looked from Hazlet to Dougal, before turning away.

Dougal said softly, "I should go with you."

"Nay." Hazlet's eyes blazed behind her veil. "Our people cannot afford to lose both of you. If you intend to follow through on this folly, nephew, you'd best leave Dougal here to reign as laird in your absence."

Grant heard the murmur of voices coming

from the great hall below stairs, where many of his most trusted men had gathered. "We have the Council. They're capable of seeing to the safety of our clan until I return."

"They're fine enough warriors, if that's all that is needed. But you said yourself there may be a traitor among them. Who can be trusted to make a decision of any importance while you're off chasing after witches?"

Grant took no offense at the hint of sarcasm that colored her words. There was a time when he, too, would have dismissed witches and magic as complete nonsense. But that was before he'd become desperate to learn the truth behind his betrayal.

He turned to his brother. "Aunt Hazlet is right, of course. Until I return, I leave the protection of our people to the Council, and any decisions requiring my seal to you, Dougal. You'll see to it?"

"If you order it, though I'd rather ride with you than stay behind."

"I order it, then."

The two men clasped hands.

"What about me, my laird? Will you at least permit me to ride with you?"

At Finlay's question, Grant looked over. "Nay, my friend. You'll stay and see to the safety of my brother and my aunt."

A short time later the three watched as Grant strode from the room. They stood together on the balcony and heard the servants shouting out words of farewell as their laird turned his steed toward the misty mountains that loomed in the distance.

Hazlet turned away, shaking her head. "Grant is as stubborn as my brother Stirling was. I only pray he doesn't prove himself to be as fool-hardy, as well."

Her words sent a shudder through Dougal. It was common knowledge that his father's reckless disregard for his own safety on the field of battle had cost him his life and that of his closest friend, Ranald, who had been the great love of Hazlet's life. Brokenhearted, Hazlet had taken to her chambers in mourning, refusing to see anyone.

To add to the family woes, Stirling's beautiful young wife, Mary, made frail by the birth of her firstborn, died hours after giving birth to Dougal. Hazlet had been forced to rouse herself from her grief to assist at the birth and care for the infant.

Seeing Dougal's distress, Hazlet was quick to soothe. "You mustn't fret, dear heart."

"But what if our family is doomed to repeat the mistakes of the past? You said yourself that Grant is reckless."

"That doesn't mean you must be like him."

"The same blood flows through our veins."

"As it flows through mine." She touched a hand to his cheek. "But I am no more like my brother than you are like yours. Come. We'll go below stairs and meet with the others. Once they learn of their laird's latest folly, they'll be in need of wise counsel. Together you and I will ease their fears."

Behind them, old Finlay remained on the balcony, watching until his laird was out of sight.

The forest was dark as midnight. No sunlight could penetrate the thick growth of twisted, tangled brush that resisted every step taken. Grant had been forced to dismount and use his sword to hack at the vines and shrubs that barred his way. Several times his steed drew back in terror as creatures swooped from above, eyes glittering like burning embers in the darkness. It was enough to chill a man's soul and fuel a raging terror. But the need that drove him consumed him far greater than any fear of the unknown. And so he plunged on, determined to reach his goal.

After many torturous hours he saw the faint glow of light ahead. At last he breathed a sigh of relief as he stepped from the forest and was almost blinded by the glare of sunlight reflecting off the water that lay directly before him.

"The Enchanted Loch." He breathed the name of the place he'd heard about since childhood. Surely it was so, since the water glistened with the colors of diamonds and sapphires. He cupped a handful and drank. It was the sweetest, purest water he'd ever tasted. When he looked down at his fingers, he saw the jewel droplets remaining. But instead of water, they were actual jewels, winking in the sunlight. Brilliant white diamonds and silver-blue sapphires. Enthralled, he wrapped them in a bit of linen and tucked them into a pocket at his waist.

At a rumble of thunder that echoed across the

sky, he looked up. Not thunder, he realized. It was the roar of the dragon that guarded the loch. The creature came up slowly from the water, looming closer and larger, until it dwarfed even the cliffs that rose up on the far side. Its body was longer than any boat, and covered with scales. The giant mouth opened. A tongue flicked out, followed by a stream of fire that had Grant diving into the sandy shore to escape being burned alive.

He felt intense heat rush past his head and watched in horror as the beast emerged from the water and lumbered toward him. His first thought was that he'd never faced such a fearsome opponent. He had often been outnumbered in battle, and had been forced to fight until there was no strength left in him. But he'd always believed he had the inner resources to win. This time, his courage would be sorely tested.

He unsheathed his sword and started forward, determined to conquer both this monster and his own fear.

The dragon reared back, resting on its tail. One giant claw lashed out. In the space of a moment Grant caught sight of razor-sharp talons that could shred a man to ribbons with a single swipe. He veered to one side, and felt the quick slice of pain as his arm was cut to the bone from shoulder to elbow. For a moment the pain dropped him to his knees as blood flowed like a river, soaking his plaid. The sword slipped from his hands. The dragon used that moment to turn wrap its tail around him, pinning his arms to his sides. Ever so slowly it began to squeeze the life from him.

Grant could barely breathe as the pressure against his chest increased until he could feel stars dancing in front of his eyes. The giant tail swished to and fro, tossing him about in a dizzying ride. He knew it was only a matter of time before he would lose consciousness. Though he no longer had his sword, he still had the dirk in his boot. He eased his foot up until his fingertips came in contact with the cold steel of the dagger. Sweat beaded his forehead as he moved the blade inch by inch, until at last he managed to grasp it firmly and began methodically cutting away at the scaly flesh that held him prisoner. With the first cut he felt his chest expand enough to breathe easily. With the second cut, and the third, he could feel himself slipping free. Another slice, and then another, and he was falling through air until he landed with a splash in the water. For a few unsteady moments he sank beneath the waves and wondered if, after all this, he might face death by drowning. But then he felt the sand beneath his feet and knew that he had reached the shallows. There, just in front of him, lay his fallen sword.

He saw the dragon rear up, and knew that he wouldn't survive a second attack. Taking up his sword, he changed course, choosing to attack rather than simply defend himself. Darting between the creature's front legs, he looked up and saw the massive pulsing chest just above him. Using both hands, he grasped his sword and drove it deep into the beast's heart.

The dragon fell back, its eyes fixed on the sun as it emitted a roar that echoed across the heavens. The water ran red with its blood as it slowly sank beneath the waves.

Grant staggered to the shore and lay struggling for breath as the Enchanted Loch stirred and bubbled, before growing calm once more. When he sat up, there was no sign of the dragon. But the water remained bloodred, glistening like rubies.

He tied a length of plaid around his arm to stem the flow of blood. With his sword at the ready, he caught his horse and led it into the loch. Whatever other dangers lay in wait for him, he would meet them with the same unflinching determination. Though he was exhausted from his battle with the monster, he was determined that nothing would keep him from his goal of reaching the Mystical Kingdom and the witches who dwelled therein.

Hearing the distant roar, Nola Drummond looked up from her loom and cast a worried glance at the sky outside her cottage. The heavens were a sea of blue, without a cloud on the horizon.

She hurried to the doorway and called out to her mother, who was cooking over an open fire. ''The dragon cries.''

''Aye.'' Wilona wiped a sheen of sweat from her brow. ''We must summon the lasses home.''

Leaving Bessie to stir the kettle, the two women started across the meadow until they reached a hill, giving them a clear view of the area around them. Lifting their fingers to their lips, they gave the whistle that had always been their signal of impending danger. Minutes later Gwenellen stepped out of the forest, trailed by the little troll, Jeremy, and hurried toward them.

Nola greeted her daughter with a hug. "Where is your sister?"

Gwenellen shrugged. "Knowing Kylia's love of the water, I'm sure she's in the loch, or near it."

Wilona saw the fear that crossed Nola's face. Drawing an arm around her daughter's shoulders, and another around her granddaughter, she said soothingly, "Have no fear. Our Kylia's not one to take foolish risks. Surely she would have heard the dragon's cry and is even now on her way to the cottage. Come." Linking hands, she led them across the meadow, with Jeremy running to keep up. All the while she prayed they would soon spy the slender figure of the one they sought awaiting them in the doorway of their home.

* * *

Kylia stared in amazement at the bloodred water that washed ashore, staining the hem of her gown. This same thing had happened not a year ago, when a stranger slew the dragon that guarded their kingdom, and forced her older sister, Allegra, to accompany him to his home. What had begun as a fearsome situation had grown into a deep and abiding love between Allegra and her beloved, Merrick MacAndrew. Now Allegra lived with him and his young son, Hamish, in Berkshire Castle, far from the Mystical Kingdom. But they returned often, and Allegra's family was assured that she had found great joy in that other world.

It had been Kylia who had later found the dragon's egg, in a nest hidden along the banks of the loch. She had watched the egg hatch, and the tiny dragon grow until it had become, like its forebears, a fierce protector of their land. She felt a heaviness around her heart, thinking about the nest she had recently found, bearing yet another egg. Had the dragon somehow sensed that its time on this earth was nearing an end?

Kylia thought about her grandmother's favor-

ite expression. *To all things there is a season.*
There was a rhythm to life, Wilona explained.
A time to live. A time to die. A time to learn.
A time to love.

When would it be her turn? Kylia thought as
the water began to churn and bubble.

As if in reply, she saw a shimmering image
beneath the waves. Gradually the image came
into focus. The face of the man she'd seen dozens of times here in the loch since her childhood. The familiar dark hair, streaming past his
shoulders. The gray eyes, deeply troubled. The
strong, firm jaw and the cleft in the chin. But
instead of fading, as it always had in the past,
it came into sharper focus and began to rise up
out of the loch.

Now there was more than a face. So much
more. There were broad, muscular shoulders
and a powerful chest, barely covered by a length
of dripping plaid. In his hand was a sword with
a jeweled hilt that caught and reflected the sunlight. His other hand gripped the reins of a horse
that followed slowly behind him.

Both man and beast appeared exhausted and
were breathing heavily.

For a moment neither the man nor Kylia spoke a word, but merely stared at each other with matching looks of surprise.

When he stepped closer, Kylia found her voice. "The fact that you were able to slay our guardian means that your strength is great, indeed, for Gram says it takes superior powers to overcome the dragon."

When he continued staring at her in silence, she felt the heat rush to her cheeks. "Forgive me. My first words to you should have been in greeting. Welcome to the Mystical Kingdom. My name is Kylia. My family is of the clan Drummond. And though your name is not known to me, your face is. For I've seen it here in the loch since I was but a child."

Grant was incredulous. The woman facing him was no witch. Here was a goddess. Skin as pale as milk. Hair as blue-black and shiny as the wings of a raven, twisted into one fat braid that fell to her waist. Such a tiny waist, tied with a ribbon into which she'd tucked a sprig of heather that matched the color of her eyes.

Her words of greeting made no sense to him. "You've seen me?"

"Aye." She spread her hands to indicate the water that was now as crystal clear and dazzling as diamonds. "Here." She looked up and her smile rivaled the sun. "I always knew one day you would come."

"You knew...?" He felt an odd buzzing in his head, and wondered why her voice was fading.

Her smile vanished. "Forgive my babbling. You're wounded."

"Am I?" He glanced idly at the blood that streamed from his throbbing arm, and started to reach for it to stem the flow of blood. Before he could move, he felt his legs fail him.

Spots danced in front of his eyes. The buzzing increased in volume until it seemed a hive of hornets had taken over his brain.

Without a word he dropped to the sand just as the sunlight disappeared from his view and he was engulfed in a tunnel of darkness.

Chapter Two

Grant lay very still, absorbing so many strange sounds and smells. Soft, muted voices. Laughter trilling as gently as music. The sweet perfume of heather, and the mouthwatering scent of meat and herbs roasting over a fire.

He lay, eyes closed, waiting for the pain he knew would come. He shifted slightly on a pallet as soft as down. In the absence of pain he touched a hand to his arm. There wasn't so much as a twinge. Nor could he feel blood or dressing or scar. His eyes snapped open and he looked around.

"So, you've finally decided to come back to us."

With a rustle of skirts the goddess knelt beside him.

He felt the jolt of recognition. "I remember you. You were on shore when I stepped from the loch. I don't recall much after that."

Her laughter rang as clear as a bell. "That's not surprising since you fell to the sand. I couldn't rouse you, so I called for my family to help."

"Where am I?"

"In our cottage." She blushed. "In my bed. You've been asleep for three days."

"Three days?"

"And three nights." Full, perfect lips parted in a smile. "But Gram said we weren't to worry, for your body craved the healing power of sleep."

"Gram?"

"I live here in the Mystical Kingdom with my mother, my grandmother, and my younger sister, as well as some friends. Jeremy, a troll, and Bessie, who is like a dear old aunt. I have an older sister, as well, but she left home to be with her new husband."

He struggled to keep up. "And your name is…Kylia?"

"You remember."

How could he forget? Never in his life had he seen such a perfect creature. "My arm..." He lifted it from the fur covering and was startled into silence. Had he only dreamed the attack by the dragon's vicious claws?

She gave another soft laugh that did strange things to his heart. "It took a great deal of chanting and conjuring to heal it. My older sister, Allegra, is the finest healer among us. But now that she's gone, we must make do with our meager gifts."

"You..." He swallowed. "You chanted away my wound?"

"It was still fresh enough that we could manage it. We had to use herbs and a great deal of meditation for some of the older scars."

"Older scars?" Beneath the covers he ran his hand over his chest and discovered that the long-familiar knots and twists of flesh were gone. His skin was now as smooth as a newborn babe's. Shocked, he started to sit up and the fur covering slipped to his waist, revealing the fact that he was naked. Though he quickly recovered and tucked the fur around himself for modesty, he could see the color spreading on Kylia's cheeks as she scrambled to her feet.

"I'll just fetch your plaid. Mum repaired it and washed the blood from it."

As she disappeared from sight, Grant lay back, feeling more than a little overwhelmed. Had he lost his senses? Or was this really happening to him?

It didn't seem possible that such a serious wound to his arm could heal within three days without leaving a mark. What was more, even older scars had disappeared, leaving his flesh without a blemish. He felt reborn. In truth, he couldn't recall ever feeling this rested. He felt a wave of momentary discomfort when he thought about strange women examining his body for scars. Still, what mattered more was that every scar had been swept away with a few spells.

He pressed an arm over his eyes and gave a long, deep sigh. Either he had gone completely mad, or the tales he'd heard for a lifetime were true and he was actually in the Mystical Kingdom, in the company of witches.

Grant tossed the plaid over one shoulder, leaving his arms and torso bare in the manner of a Highlander. As he stepped from the cottage, he felt the warmth of the sun on his face and paused a moment to enjoy the view.

A variety of women in gaily-colored gowns were involved in diverse activities. A woman with long, dark hair threaded with gray stood beside a fire, stirring something in a cauldron. But this was no witch's brew. The wonderful scent wafting on the breeze had his mouth watering. To one side was a younger woman, working a loom. A hunched, older woman was seated at her feet, twisting the yarn, gathering it into a skein. And approaching from the loch was a little troll who had to be Jeremy, as well as a blue-eyed, golden-haired waif striding alongside Kylia, holding a string of fish.

They called out, "Good day to you."

"Good day." He paused. "I thank you all for your gift of healing. I am forever in your debt."

The older woman smiled. "We were pleased to be of service. I am Wilona, of the clan Drummond." She turned to a woman seated at a loom. "This is my daughter, Nola, and our friend, Bessie. This is Jeremy, and my granddaughters Gwenellen and Kylia, whom you've already met."

He tried not to stare at the raven-haired beauty, whose damp gown clung to every line and curve of her slender body. She seemed completely unaware of how she looked as she picked up a sharp knife and began preparing the fish for the fire.

"I am Grant, laird of the clan MacCallum."

"A laird?" Wilona gave him an assessing look. "We are honored by your visit. But a man doesn't pit his courage against a dragon without good reason. What does the laird of the clan MacCallum desire from the Mystical Kingdom?"

He thought of the bitter betrayal that had brought him to such a desperate journey. His tone hardened. "I come seeking the name of my enemy, who walks in the guise of friend."

"What makes you think we can help you?"

"You have already proved that you can heal my body. I must heal my clan by learning a name."

"So that you can seek vengeance?"

He heard the note of censure in the old woman's voice. "So that I can keep my people safe from future betrayals."

Wilona studied him before turning back to the kettle. "There is time to speak of this later. For now, since you've regained your strength, Kylia and Gwenellen are eager to show you our kingdom."

Grant knew that he was being dismissed, yet he took no offense. These women needed time to allay their fears of him, just as he needed time to adjust to his situation. "I'm eager to see it, for I've heard of this place since I was a wee bairn."

He followed slowly behind the two young women who danced ahead, leading their guest across a meadow abloom with heather. Jeremy, no taller than a lad, trailed far behind.

When they were gone, Wilona turned and saw her daughter watching their departure with a look of intense concentration. "You're worried, my daughter."

"Not so much worried, but…concerned."

"You fear the stranger has brought danger to our door?"

"Nay. At least not physical danger. But he is most pleasant to look upon. I've seen the way Kylia watches him."

"She's unaccustomed to having a man to look at."

"Aye. Or having a man look at her. I see him watching her, as well."

"What is it you fear, daughter? That you'll lose her to him?"

Nola was quick to shake her head. "If it were to be a love match, I would be greatly pleased. But ever since Allegra left our kingdom, I've seen a look in Kylia's eyes. She yearns for someone of her own. Someone to touch her heart in that same way Merrick has touched Allegra's heart."

"And you fear that Kylia is in love with the notion of love."

Nola nodded. "Perhaps we were wrong to shelter the lasses from the outside world. They're so innocent."

"But not helpless. We've raised them to be strong and bright and independent. Now we must trust that we gave them all they need to survive. In our world or the other."

Nola sighed. "I suppose it has always been a mother's lot in life to trust that she did all that was necessary to help her children survive and thrive."

Wilona drew an arm around her shoulders. "Come. Leave your loom for now, Nola. And your worries, as well. With Bessie's help, let's prepare a meal fit for a lord."

Grant followed the two young women across a meadow abloom with wildflowers, the likes of which he'd never seen before. Acre upon acre of foxglove taller than his head, in the most vivid shades of red and orange and deep purple. The air was perfumed with heather and soft pink roses and exotic flowers unfamiliar to him.

High in the branches of a tree the glint of sunlight caught his eye and he looked up to see tiny creatures flitting from leaf to leaf. He stopped in midstride to stare.

"Do you see them?" he called.

Kylia and Gwenellen paused to look where he pointed.

"Fairies," Kylia said matter-of-factly. "The woods are filled with them. They love to play among the leaves."

"Fairies." He stood perfectly still while the two sisters walked ahead. Then, seeing Jeremy watching him, he followed behind.

When he caught up with them they were standing on a hillside, whistling through their fingers. Minutes later two winged horses came flying overhead and landed gently in the grass, tucking their wings close to their heaving sides.

"Flying horses?" He knew his jaw had dropped, but he couldn't contain his excitement as he hurried toward them. "Do they let you ride them?"

"Aye." Kylia ran a hand over the muzzle of a coal-black horse with silver-tipped wings. "This is Moonlight. She's been mine since I was but a wee lass." She pointed to the white steed Gwenellen was mounting. "That's Starlight. And this third, Sunlight—" she watched as a lovely golden horse glided to a halt beside the little troll "—belongs to our sister Allegra. In her stead, Jeremy rides with us."

Grant shook his head in admiration as Jeremy and Gwenellen took to the air on their winged horses. "What I wouldn't give for such a wondrous thing."

Kylia touched a hand to his sleeve. "I'm truly sorry that our steeds are too small to carry you on their backs."

Grant absorbed a jolt at her touch and closed a hand over hers. "You've no need to apologize, Kylia. It's enough that I can see such a mythical creature." Because the heat was threatening to scorch him, he released her hand and moved away to pet the horse. But the tingling remained.

As for Kylia, she stood perfectly still, wondering at the heat that rushed through her at the simple touch. Would she feel the same way if touched by any man? Or was it just this man who caused such feelings?

To cover her confusion, she lifted her head and shielded her eyes from the sun. "Look how high Gwenellen and Jeremy have flown."

Grant followed her lead and looked to the heavens, stunned to see little more than two dark spots on the horizon. "How high can these creatures fly?"

She laughed. "I know not. We've never taken them to their limits."

"You mean they might be able to reach the sun?"

Kylia shrugged and, feeling another rush of heat, quickly looked away. "Who's to say where they might fly if we asked them?"

Just then a gust of wind blew across the meadow, sending the flowers in a wild dance, flattening her skirts against her legs. Looking up, she saw Gwenellen struggling to catch the reins that had been blown from her grasp.

Kylia lifted her hands, palms up, and said in a haughty tone, "I command you, be still, lest my sister take a spill."

At once a strange calm settled over the land.

While Grant watched in amazement, Gwenellen caught up the reins and the winged horse took a circular route to the ground, settling in the grass beside Jeremy, who was just dismounting.

Gwenellen's cheeks were the color of ripe apples. "That was quite a ride. Especially when that breeze caught us by surprise. Thank you, Kylia."

Her older sister gave her a quick hug. "You're welcome. You'd have taken care of it yourself, but I could see that you had other things on your mind."

"Aye. And we all know that my spells often go awry." She turned away. "We'd best get back to the cottage. Oh." She clapped a hand over her mouth. "I almost forgot. I promised Mum I'd bring her a bouquet of wildflowers for the table." She spread her arms wide and called, "Foxglove, roses, lilies, too, come and fill my arms with you."

There was a flutter of breeze and she looked in disgust at the mass of sticky chopped vegetables in her arms. "Not stew. I didn't want stew."

Kylia didn't know what tickled her more. The look in her sister's eyes, or the mass of wilted vegetables in her arms. With a laugh she clapped her hands, then spread her arms wide. In the blink of an eye she was holding an exquisite bouquet of wildflowers, which she handed to her little sister. "Here you are. I believe this will be more to your liking."

"Thank you." Gwenellen turned to Grant. "I hope you're hungry."

He wondered if these three could read the astonishment in his eyes as he followed them across the meadow toward the distant cottage.

Did they know what an amazing paradise this was? Or did they believe, since they'd lived here all their lives, that everyone enjoyed such comfort?

It occurred to Grant that if the outside world had any idea just what lay beyond the shores of the Enchanted Loch, there would be hundreds of warriors lined up to take on the dragon and any other beast that barred their way.

Chapter Three

Candles cast an inviting glow over those gathered around the table. Across the room a fire blazed on the hearth. The air that wafted through the windows was perfumed with the scent of heather and roses and all manner of exotic flowers that grew in profusion around the cottage.

Grant leaned back, feeling more content than he could ever remember. ''That was a fine meal.''

''I'm glad it pleased you.'' Wilona filled goblets with hot mulled wine and passed a plate of biscuits drizzled with honey and nuts. ''Now that you've had a chance to see some of our kingdom, what do you think?''

He sipped his wine. "It's even better than anything I could have imagined. The stories told in our land don't do it justice." He chuckled. "From the winged horses to the tiny fairies flitting from branch to branch in the trees, it's simply beyond belief. And yet I saw them, and touched them."

"And would have ridden Starlight," Gwenellen interrupted, "if you were a bit smaller."

Grant nodded at the young woman with the pixie smile. "What I wouldn't give to ride a winged horse. To fly across the sky…" His voice trailed off before he mentally shook himself. "I saw things today I never would have believed. And if I were to tell such tales in my homeland, the people would scoff."

"Such as?" Nola looked up.

"I saw Kylia fill her sister's arms with exotic flowers, the likes of which I've never seen in my land, yet she didn't pick them, but simply willed them into her hands."

"I could have done it myself if I could just get the proper words," Gwenellen said with a shrug.

"What's more, I watched Kylia calm the wind with a stern command."

"I wasn't stern." Kylia tilted her head in challenge. "I'm never stern."

"Perhaps. But the command seemed stern enough to me. And to the wind, which," he added with a laugh, "went dead calm as soon as you spoke."

That had everyone laughing.

Still chuckling, Grant spread his hands. "This place is truly paradise. And the lot of you have gifts beyond the realm of my world."

Wilona found herself smiling at the easy camaraderie that seemed to have developed between these three young people. "We feel privileged with our gifts and our dwelling place. Perhaps you would consent to stay awhile, so that you can see all that our kingdom has to offer."

He sighed. "If only I could. But I came here seeking the name of a traitor." He stared down into his goblet, as though searching for truth in the depths of his wine. "I have been betrayed by someone close to me. Someone who will do whatever it takes to defeat and disgrace me. Someone who has no regard for the pain being inflicted on innocent people." He looked up and met the old woman's eyes. "You asked earlier if I would use that knowledge for revenge. And I ask you. Could I knowingly permit such a person to continue to harm my people? Vengeance may not be mine to take, but I will not look the other way if I can put a stop to it."

Wilona glanced around the table. "Most men seek wealth or power. Do you not covet such things, my lord?"

Grant shrugged. "I share my wealth with my people. In good times and bad, whatever is mine is theirs."

"A noble deed, but one expected of a lord. And does not your title laird of the MacCallum clan imply power?"

He smiled. "The one chosen lord must be willing to fight to the death to keep his people free. I've given my word that I will do all in my power to honor that pledge. But that is the only power I seek, or shall ever desire. I have no wish to wield my power over others."

Wilona found herself warming to this young warrior. There was a dignity and honor about him that touched her heart. "Tell me. This truth you seek. What if learning it should bring you even greater heartache?"

"Why should it?"

"You could learn that you are being betrayed by one near and dear to you."

He frowned, considering the possibility. "I come seeking the truth. If that knowledge brings pain, so be it. I will have to be strong enough to bear it."

Wilona smiled. "So what you're really requesting is wisdom and insight along with truth. Do you agree?"

He returned her smile. "Call it what you will, my lady." He got to his feet and bowed to the others. "By your leave I go now to see to my steed. I must return to my people on the morrow."

"So soon?" Kylia clapped a hand over her mouth when she realized that everyone had turned to look at her.

Grant gave her a gentle smile. "My lady, my people have been without my protection long enough." He walked from the cottage.

Almost at once Kylia excused herself and slipped away to the privacy of her room. Minutes later Gwenellen followed.

Seeing the way Nola was staring at the closed door, Wilona drew an arm around her.

"You see?" Nola looked into her mother's eyes. "It's as I feared. Already Kylia is mourning the loss of this stranger."

"It's only natural." The older woman ran a hand down her daughter's hair. "We've had so few visitors to our kingdom. You can't blame Kylia for wanting this young lord to stay."

"Nay. I can't." Nola stared at the floor. "But our loneliness and isolation will seem all the more when he is gone and Kylia finds herself alone with only Gwenellen for company."

Wilona sighed and patted her daughter's hand. "What will be will be. We'll face the morrow when it comes."

Nola walked to the window of the cottage and watched the silhouette of the man tending his horse by moonlight. In her heart of hearts she knew the morrow would come far too soon to suit her.

The sky was barely streaked with fingers of dawn before the members of the household were awake and seeing to their morning chores.

Jeremy added fresh wood to the fire, while Wilona lifted perfectly baked scones and Bessie stirred a bowl of still-warm fruit preserves. Nola put the finishing touches on a gown of soft cream wool that she'd been stitching for Gwen-ellen. The two sisters returned to the cottage, giggling over secrets and carrying a basket of eggs between them.

Grant paused in the doorway of the cottage and felt the quick tug at his heart when he caught sight of Kylia. She was unlike any maiden he'd ever known. There was a shyness, a sweetness about her that set her apart from the women in his world. And yet, for all her inno-cence, she seemed aware of him in a womanly way. He'd felt the heat whenever they touched, and sensed that she felt it, too. But though she did nothing to encourage him, neither did she discourage him. She was a strange one. He wished he had more time to stay and figure her out. But he had an obligation to his people. As much as he loved seeing her world, it was time to return to his.

He stepped out into the morning sunshine and breathed in the sweet, fresh air.

"Good morrow, my lord." Wilona set aside her spoon and dried her hands on a square of linen. "How did you sleep?"

"Well enough." In truth, he'd been beset by strange dreams, seeing the faces of family and friends, all turned against him.

"We will break our fast now," Wilona announced, leading the way inside.

Grant shrugged aside his unsettling thoughts and followed her. At the table he sipped a goblet of mulled wine and nibbled eggs and scones slathered with fruit conserve.

"You seem distracted, my lord. Is the food not to your liking?"

He turned to Wilona. "Forgive me, my lady. My thoughts are on those I left behind."

"Have you a wife, my lord? A family?"

Across the table, Kylia held her breath.

He shook his head. "There is only my brother, Dougal."

Kylia felt a hand on hers, and looked over to see Gwenellen smiling. A matching smile stole over her own lips.

"There is also an elderly aunt, Hazlet." Grant found himself staring at Kylia's mouth. Even from this distance he could feel the warmth of that sweet smile. "She was sister to my father, and serves as mistress of my home."

"Did your aunt never wed?"

"Nay. She lost her heart to a warrior, who was killed on the field of battle. She chose to live alone rather than love another."

Nola felt her daughters' glances and lowered her head. Though her husband Kenneth Drummond had been gone since she was ten and nine, she missed him still. Some would consider her life a lonely one. She felt no such loneliness, for she had her memories to comfort her. And much preferred them to a flesh-and-blood man who could never take the place of her Kenneth.

The silence was broken as Grant set aside his goblet. "You know the favor I seek. Which of you will be gracious enough to give me the name of my enemy?"

Wilona turned and fixed her middle granddaughter with a look. "It is Kylia's gift to see the soul through a person's eyes. If anyone can identify the one who betrays you, it is she."

Grant pushed away from the table and dropped to his knees before Kylia, bowing his head. "You healed my wounds, my lady. Now I ask that you heal the wounds of my people by revealing the name of my enemy."

Kylia was aware of the way her family was watching, but all she could see was this man, this mighty lord and warrior, bowing humbly before her to ask a favor. A favor that only she could grant.

She placed a hand on either side of his face and lifted it until she was looking into his eyes. She was jolted by the sadness revealed in their depths. Hadn't she seen this man and his sorrow since she was but a child? She believed with all her heart that he had been fated to come here, just as she had been fated to be here awaiting his arrival in her kingdom.

"Your pain touches me deeply, Lord MacCallum. I promise to do my best to learn the name of the one who betrays you."

He caught her hands in his and pressed a kiss to each palm. "I thank you, my lady. And I await your word."

At the touch of his lips to her flesh, Kylia's eyes widened and she was forced to absorb a rush of heat that left her shaken to her very core. She shook her head. "You misunderstand, my lord. I cannot simply look into your eyes and see all that you desire. There is but one way for me to recognize your enemy."

"And how is that?"

"By looking into his eyes."

It took him a moment to realize what she was saying. "You would willingly leave this paradise and accompany me to my home?"

"I know of no other way to discern your enemy, my lord."

He seemed overwhelmed by her words. "You realize I must leave within the hour."

She nodded. "I'll make ready to leave, as well."

"Nay. It's too soon." Nola pushed away from the table, unable to stop the words of protest that sprang to her lips.

Everyone turned to look at her.

She clasped her hands together and stared at the floor. "You're far too young to consider leaving home, Kylia."

"At my age you were wed and had three children, Mother."

"But you've led a sheltered life. You're ill prepared for the world beyond our shores."

"Perhaps. But I'll learn, as Allegra learned. As you and Gram learned." Kylia turned pleading eyes to her grandmother. "What good are our gifts if we have no chance to use them? Aren't we being selfish if we keep ourselves hidden away here, when there are those in need of us in that other world beyond our shores?''

''What about me?'' Gwenellen caught her sister's hand and felt tears well up. She blinked hard to keep them from spilling over. ''How can you leave me here alone, Kylia?''

''You could come with me.''

The young girl shook her head sadly. ''I can't leave Mum and Gram.'' Her lips pursed into a pout. ''Please don't leave me, Kylia. What will I do with both you and Allegra far away?''

Her sister gathered her close. Against her temple, she whispered, ''I shall miss you terribly. But I must do this, don't you see? I believe it is my fate to do so.''

Nola gripped the back of the chair and studied her middle daughter as though memorizing every line and curve of that lovely face. ''Can you not give us a few more days?''

Kylia turned to Grant, who had watched and listened in silence.

He squared his shoulders. ''I wish it could be so. I've been gone long enough. I must return to my people now.''

Kylia nodded. "Then I go with you. Now."

As they started toward the door, Nola picked up a heavy traveling cloak and draped it around her daughter's shoulders.

Kylia paused and turned.

Nola managed a weak smile as she lifted a hand to the fasteners. "I was just your age when I wore this. You'll have need of it. The weather in that other world is not as gentle as ours."

Kylia wrapped her arms around her mother's neck and hugged her fiercely. After, without a word she embraced her grandmother, then her sister, before pausing to hug Bessie and Jeremy.

She stepped out the door where Grant was holding the reins of his steed.

He paused a moment to look down into her upturned face. "You're sure of this?"

She nodded, too overcome by the enormity of what she was doing to speak. There was a lump in her throat the size of a rock.

He lifted her to the saddle, then pulled himself up behind her. With a quick salute to her family, he flicked the reins and the horse took off at a run.

As the horse and its riders crested a hill, the

three women stretched out their hands to one another and formed a circle. As they began to chant the ancient words, Kylia lifted her head. Even above the sound of splashing as the horse entered the Enchanted Loch, she could hear the words clearly. As the water rose, she rolled her cloak into a bundle and tied it behind the saddle before slipping into the water. Grant was amazed by the ease with which she swam, easily keeping pace beside him. With each powerful stroke, he thought he heard chanting.

By the time they'd reached the far shore, he could hear the chanting inside his mind. And though the words were foreign to him, he found them oddly soothing.

"You'll need this to keep warm until your gown dries, my lady." He unrolled her cloak and draped it around her. As he did, he felt the quick jolt. Though he'd prepared himself for it, it still managed to catch him off guard. He allowed his hand to linger as he lifted the hood and tucked her wet hair inside.

"Thank you, my lord." She looked up at him with a heart-stopping smile.

Perhaps it was the smile. Or the anticipation

of returning to his home. Or the fact that he'd
wanted to taste her lips since the first time he'd
seen her. Whatever the reason, he lowered his
head to her and brushed his mouth over hers.

He'd meant it to be no more than a simple
touch of lips to lips. The merest whisper of butterfly wings. But the minute their mouths
touched, mated, everything changed.

Here was more than mere heat. This was an
inferno that had the blood roaring in his temples
as he drank in the sweetness of her. Such goodness, it flowed through her and into him, warming him as nothing else ever had. The mere
touch of her mouth left him stunned and reeling.

He needed to touch her. He allowed his hand
to move slowly down her back, drawing her
even closer, until he could feel her heartbeat inside his own chest.

He knew he'd overstepped his bounds, but
now that he was holding her, kissing her, he
couldn't seem to stop. There was unbelievable
sweetness here. Innocence. And just beneath
that, a hint of awakening passion.

What would it be like to lose himself in her?
To take and give until they were both sated?

As for Kylia, she felt herself sinking sweetly into the kiss as though coming home. Hadn't she known it would be like this? She'd seen this man's face, looked into those eyes, since she was a lass. She thought she knew him so well. But kissing him was something more. So very much more. She felt the heat, the need, and then the long, deep tug of desire.

Oh, she didn't know him at all. This wasn't just a face, a smile. This was heat and energy and the most amazing blur of color and scent and sound, swirling wildly inside her mind. What she saw, what she felt, left her dizzy and more than a little breathless.

When he heard her moan he stepped back, breaking contact.

As he did, the chanting he'd been hearing in his mind suddenly ceased.

He lifted Kylia to the saddle, then pulled himself up behind her and flicked the reins. Horse and riders shivered at the coolness of the air that surrounded them like a shroud.

Chapter Four

As soon as they could no longer see any sign of the Mystical Kingdom, Kylia fell ominously silent.

Grant tried to imagine what it must be like for her. She had, after all, spent a lifetime in a world far removed from this. She had no concept of hatred or jealousy or warfare. For all of her years she had known only tenderness and kindness and love. And isolation. What would it be like for her to see the many people of his clan? To try to live among them while she sorted out the ones who were loyal and those who would betray him?

Was she already regretting her decision to defy her mother and leave her paradise? He tried to think of something to say that might cheer her.

As the horse picked its way through a steep, narrow trail clogged with boulders, Grant leaned forward. "This would be the ideal time to whistle up your winged horse, my lady."

She pulled herself back from her thoughts and shivered at the warmth of his breath. She couldn't ignore the little curl of pleasure along her spine. "With Moonlight at our disposal, we would already be in your Highland lair, my lord."

"We'd certainly have the attention of all my people. I'm not sure they'd believe even after seeing it." He touched a hand to her arm. "Are you weary? Would you care to stop and rest?"

Oddly touched by his concern, she shook her head. "I know you're eager to return to your—" At the stomp and whinny of a horse nearby, her head came up sharply. "It would seem we're not alone."

He reined in his mount, for he, too, had heard it. Before he could dismount, the branches of the evergreens around them seemed alive with men slipping from their places of concealment. All were brandishing weapons.

In the blink of an eye Grant had an arm around her waist, lowering her to the ground while shouting, "Run to the cover of the forest!"

Then, seeking to distract the strangers while she escaped, he withdrew his sword and urged his mount forward until he was surrounded by armed men.

Kylia was forced to watch in horror as he plunged into the thick of danger, his blade slashing with deadly accuracy.

For one who had never seen battle, it was awesome to behold a lone warrior standing against more than a dozen fierce-looking barbarians. Some screamed like banshees while others cursed or grunted as they attacked. Though Grant was a skilled warrior, able to dance aside, avoiding the most deadly lunges, the sheer number of attackers began to take their toll on him. The blade of a sword found his shoulder. The tip of a knife his thigh. An arrow sang through the air and pierced his side with a sickening thud.

Though he was bleeding from half a dozen wounds, he continued fighting against the armed men who came at him in waves.

Suddenly a voice rose above the others. "Highlander, lay down your weapon, or the woman dies."

Grant turned to see Kylia in the clutches of one of the barbarians. A brawny arm was wrapped around her waist, a knife pressed to her throat, already drawing blood from a cut to her tender flesh.

"I'll do as you ask. Don't harm the woman." Grant lowered his hand. The moment his sword fell to the ground, his attackers were on him like a pack of hungry dogs.

While several of them held his arms behind him, the others slashed and beat and kicked. Helpless to defend himself, he absorbed wave after wave of pain until, at a word from their leader, he was released and allowed to collapse in a bloody heap on the ground.

The one who was holding Kylia stepped closer, dragging her with him. "Laird Grant MacCallum, now will ye die far from yer home, ne'er to see it or those ye love again."

"How do you know my name?"

"We were told to await yer arrival. There is one among yer people who wishes ye dead."

As he raised his sword, Kylia used that moment of distraction to pull free of his grasp.

Instead of fleeing, she turned to face him, lifting both her arms high above her head. With the long hooded cape flowing around her, and the tall grass swaying at her feet, she was a fearsome sight.

For a moment the barbarians seemed more stunned than angry. But when she began chanting in an ancient tongue, they turned to their leader for guidance.

"A witch," he shouted. "Kill her quickly, before she's able to call down her magic to be used against us."

Several of the men started toward her, then suddenly dropped to their knees as though frozen. Their weapons slipped from their hands.

"Get up, fools. Seize the woman."

When they refused their leader's command, he waved to several more who leaped over their comrades, only to find themselves similarly frozen on their knees, their weapons littering the ground.

"Witch. Now will ye pay." With his dirk uplifted, the leader stepped over Grant's body and started toward her.

"You cannot harm me." Her gaze narrowed on him. Her eyes glowed with an inner fire. She fixed him with a look that had the blood chilling in his veins.

"Ye'll not stop…" The words died on his lips as he sank to his knees. His blade dropped in the grass.

Keeping her arms uplifted, Kylia turned to Grant, lying so still and lifeless on the ground. "My lord, you must help me if we're to make good our escape."

In reply he moaned softly.

Her heart lay heavy in her chest.

She stepped closer until her skirts were brushing his bloody face. "My lord MacCallum. Stay here with me. Keep your mind focused. You must not let the pain take you down."

He looked up, struggling to make out her form through the haze that blurred his vision. Why was she holding her arms aloft? And where were the barbarians? He glanced around and saw them, kneeling like statues around her. "What is it you wish of me?"

"I wish you to stand. But I cannot help you, for if I lower my arms, the spell that holds these warriors captive will be broken."

He reached a hand to her skirts, pulling himself to a sitting position, and waited for the dizziness to fade. Then slowly, painfully, through the sheer force of his will, he got to his knees, then to his feet, before wrapping his arms around her waist to keep from falling.

His horse stood by the entrance to the forest nibbling grass. No more than a few dozen strides, but to Grant it seemed an impossible distance to cross. He could no more manage it than he could climb a Highland mountain or swim the North Channel.

"Hold on to me, my lord." Kylia began leading him in slow, baby steps, and could feel him tremble with each painful movement. As he walked, the blood flowed freely, soaking his plaid. Sweat beaded his forehead, revealing the effort it cost him.

It would seem he had no choice but to go where she led him. Not that he minded for, in truth, he wanted desperately to leave this place. If only his body would obey his mind.

When they reached his steed he clung to the saddle for long minutes, breathing deeply. Kylia could see that he hadn't the strength left to mount. And yet, if she should lower her arms to help him, they would be forced to face the wrath of the barbarians.

She looked around and spotted a fallen tree nearby. ''Lean on your steed, my lord. We must go a bit farther.''

Holding to the saddle, Grant stumbled along beside her until they reached the logs. With the added height he was able to pull himself onto the back of his horse. For Kylia, mounting would be almost as difficult as if she were wounded.

She climbed to the top of the tallest log in the pile and balanced herself there before sprinting into the saddle. At the same instant, Grant locked his arms around her waist and took up the reins. As the horse stepped into the cool, dark forest, she lowered her arms, which had lost all feeling, and breathed a sigh of relief.

''How do you know the barbarians won't follow, my lady?''

''When they awaken from their spell, there will be confusion. If they should decide to follow, they'll surely choose another direction, for there are few who would dare to enter the Forest of Darkness.''

"I can't say I blame them." He could feel the darkness closing in as the horse moved deeper into the forest. A thick, oppressive blackness that threatened to take him down. But was it this cursed place, or the effect of his wounds?

He closed his eyes against the pain and leaned forward, pressing his weight on her. His breathing was labored, his flesh hot to the touch. "Forgive me, my lady. I truly desire to stay with you, to see you through this fearsome place. But I can feel myself slipping away."

Alarmed, Kylia reined in their mount and slid from the saddle. As she reached up, Grant tumbled into her arms and the two of them fell to the ground in a heap of twisted arms and legs. While she struggled to untangle herself, Kylia realized that Grant had lapsed into unconsciousness. When at last she managed to free herself from his body, she fumbled around in the darkness until she found the horse's reins. Tying the animal firmly to a nearby tree to keep it from bolting, she wrapped Grant in her traveling cloak, then began feeling around the ground for sticks. Because she was too impatient to waste the time it would take to rub the sticks together until they created heat, she used an incantation to bring the fire. Soon the sticks were ablaze, offering not only heat, but blessed light in the darkness. Enough light to tend Grant's wounds.

So many wounds. How had he managed to remain standing through such cruel punishment?

While chanting the ancient words she traced a fingertip over his shoulder, his thigh, his waist, commanding the bleeding to cease and the flesh to begin its long journey toward healing.

Her voice grew hoarse. Still, she continued chanting, knowing that if she stopped, this man could be plunged into crisis, for he'd sustained far too many wounds for his body to recover.

Her eyes grew heavy and she longed to sleep. Still she continued feeding the fire to hold the darkness at bay. Each time her head bobbed, she jerked awake and stood, shaking down her skirts and walking around the clearing, gathering more wood for the fire. Having successfully fought off the weariness for another hour, she would then kneel and continue the chanting that was required for healing.

Grant lay very still, fighting his way back from the darkness that had overtaken him.

Though there was pain, it wasn't nearly as searing as it had been earlier, when he'd felt himself close to death.

He could hear the hiss and snap of the fire nearby, and the sound of Kylia's voice chanting the ancient words. He found them oddly soothing. In fact, just knowing she was here with him had him feeling easy in his mind.

How magnificent she'd been when she'd stood up to their attackers. Though it must have been a shock to her tender sensibilities to find herself at the mercy of barbarians, she'd betrayed not a trace of fear.

What an unforgettable introduction she'd been given to his world. He regretted that he couldn't have been more help to her. It shamed him to know that, though he'd been the one trained as a warrior, a protector of women and children, it had fallen instead to this sweet, sheltered woman to protect him.

He felt the touch of her hand on his flesh and was warmed by it. As her fingertips moved in a circular motion over his shoulder, he could feel the pain beginning to subside.

He thought about opening his eyes, but it

seemed too great an effort. And so he lay, allowing her touch to soothe and heal. From across the clearing came the stomp and whinny of his steed. Somewhere nearby a night bird called out in a high, shrill whistle.

He drifted off, lulled by the sounds of the night. Sometime later he awoke and realized the chanting had ceased. He felt something soft and warm and opened his eyes to find Kylia curled up beside him, sound asleep.

She made such a pretty picture in the firelight. Dark hair spilling around that sweet, heart-shaped face. Her hands resting lightly on his arm, as though determined, even in sleep, to continue her healing touch and permit nothing to break the connection between them.

Then he saw the thin line of blood along her throat, where the barbarian's blade had cut her tender flesh. He felt a blaze of fury that anyone could willingly harm such a gentle creature. With a muttered oath he touched a finger to the spot and realized that, though the blood had dried, her flesh had already healed itself.

He was nearly overcome with relief.

Moving carefully so as not to wake her, he

lifted a corner of the traveling cloak and tucked it around her. In her sleep she sighed and snuggled closer.

He absorbed the most amazing heat and lay for long moments, watching her sleep.

How was it that he had been given the good fortune to come across this woman? Angel or witch, it mattered not to him. What did matter was that she was willing to sacrifice everything she'd ever known for a man she'd only met. Would he have done as much? He had no answer to that. He knew only that whenever he looked at this woman, he felt drawn to her in a way he'd never been drawn to any other.

She'd told him that she had been seeing his face since she was but a lass. Did that mean they were fated to be together?

Too many questions, he thought. And all of them puzzling to the point of being vexing.

Unable to keep his eyes open any longer, he gave in to the exhaustion that drained him. And joined her in sleep.

Chapter Five

Kylia awoke to find herself cradled in Grant's arms, her head pillowed on his shoulder, her hands resting against his heart. She could feel the strong, steady beat of it keeping time to her own.

Never in her life had she felt so intimately connected to another. As if their heartbeats were one. As if even their breathing moved, slow and steady, in perfect rhythm.

She looked up to find him watching her. Her cheeks bloomed with color.

"Good morrow, my lady." Her found her embarrassment oddly appealing. It was obvious that she was neither coy nor flirtatious, but simply out of her element and scrambling to find her way.

"Good morrow." She tried to pull away and found herself firmly bound by his arms. "How do you feel?"

"Much better than I'd expected to feel after battling the barbarians. Whatever spell you cast over me, my lady, I am grateful."

"It was no spell. I merely called upon your body to heal itself."

He chuckled. "I've often called upon my body to do things it resisted. This is the first I can recall that it actually obeyed."

At the sound of his laughter, she experienced a strange curling sensation deep inside. Was this something men and women often felt? Or was this something that only she could feel? She'd never before been so confused, and trying with all her might not to let that confusion show.

She struggled to keep her tone light. "That's because no one taught you the words."

He stared into her eyes and felt the most amazing rush of heat. "I woke once and heard you chanting. But the words were unknown to me."

"It is the lost language of our ancestors."

"If it's lost, how do you know it?"

"My mother and grandmother have kept it alive for my sisters and me. It will be up to us to see that it is preserved for future generations." She pushed herself up and sat facing him. "Now, if you don't mind, I'll tend to your wounds. I should have done this last night. Alas, I fell asleep."

"An annoying human habit." Her hair, dark as midnight, swirled forward as she bent to him. He wondered if she had any idea what her touch was doing to him. A quick glance at her face showed the depth of her concentration. It nearly made him laugh aloud. Here he was, completely aroused, while she was oblivious to all but his wounds.

He tucked a strand of hair behind her ear. "You'd make a fine physician, my lady."

She continued probing, running her fingers over the flesh of his shoulder until she saw him wince. "Sorry. My sister Allegra is much better at this than I. I can tell that wound will need some time before it's completely healed. Can you bear the pain?"

"It's tolerable. Besides, when you touch me like this, I forget all about the pain."

She glanced down and saw the dangerous smile curving his lips. "Forgive me." Her heart took a quick dip and she abruptly withdrew her hand.

"Nay, my lady." He caught her hand in his and continued holding it while her cheeks turned as red as the coals of the fire. "I enjoy teasing you."

She touched a hand to her cheek. It was, indeed, warm. And there was no denying the smile that matched his. "Am I also allowed to indulge in this teasing?"

"By all means." His grin was quick and disarming. "Though I doubt you could make me blush."

Again that quick touch of her palm to her cheek. "I shall have to ponder this awhile, my lord." She got to her feet. "Now I must find more wood for the fire, or we'll soon be mired in darkness."

He watched her walk away and wondered at the lightness around his heart. He'd been wounded by barbarians, and was confined to the Forest of Darkness, a place feared by all Highlanders. And here he was feeling like a lovesick lad with nothing more pressing than a stroll with his lass on market day. But this was no country lass. Though he had no doubt that she was as human as he, there was about her an other worldliness that both troubled and tantalized him. How could she know so much about some things while knowing so little about others? She seemed not at all uncomfortable examining his body for wounds, and yet she reacted with growing passion to his simplest touch.

He had no doubt that she was an innocent. A maiden completely unfamiliar with the ways of men and women. That only made her more appealing. But though he found himself wanting her, he felt an obligation to her family to return her as he'd found her. Untouched. Unsullied by the things of his world.

It was easy enough to resolve to do the right thing. Now if only he could remind his body to cooperate.

He closed his eyes and let himself drift on a sea of contentment. Another day of rest and he would surely be strong enough to ride. In no time they would be back in his Highland fortress. And the lovely Kylia would begin the quest for the one who betrayed him.

That was why she had agreed to accompany him to his home. He must keep her mission clearly in mind.

He must have slept, for when he opened his eyes, Kylia was cooking something over the fire. The wonderful fragrance perfumed the air.

He sat up, feeling the world spin for a moment before coming slowly into focus.

At once she looked over and, seeing him awake, hurried to kneel by his side. "How do you feel, my lord?"

"Much refreshed. But I beg your forgiveness, my lady. I've left you alone to do all the things I should be seeing to."

She shook her head, sending midnight curls dancing. "You needed to rest. Besides, I've enjoyed testing my skill. While visiting the stream, the fish fairly jumped into my net."

"Your net?" He looked around. "What did you use?"

Again that quick rush of color to her cheeks before she looked down, avoiding his eyes. "I used my petticoat."

"Your…" He burst into laughter, which only had her blush deepening.

She got to her feet and started away.

Grant sat up, thinking to follow, only to discover that beneath the cloak he was naked. "Where is my plaid?"

"I'll fetch it." She hurried away and removed it from a low-hanging branch. As she approached she explained, "It was soaked with your blood. I had to scrub it with sand several times before I managed to get it clean."

"That was kind of you." He accepted it from her hands and began winding it around his waist, before standing to toss the end over his shoulder. When he saw her watching he couldn't resist adding, "Perhaps next time you'll allow me to undress you and wash your garments, my lady."

For a moment she seemed startled. Then she spotted the gleam of laughter in his eyes. "Is this more of your teasing, my lord?"

He swallowed back the chuckle that threatened. "Aye, my lady. Forgive me. But I dearly love teasing you."

"So it would seem." She removed a stick from the fire on which had been threaded chunks of fish that were perfectly browned. "I believe you should eat something. Otherwise you'll not have the strength to tease me further.''

"That would be most unfortunate, my lady. For I've begun to dearly love the color that comes to your cheeks. It's most becoming."

She helped herself to a second stick threaded with fish, settling herself in the grass beside the fire. Moments later Grant dropped down next to her. "I wonder why my people have always feared the Forest of Darkness. It seems not at all the inhospitable place I've always heard about."

"That's because we have a fire." Seeing his arched brow, she explained, "The fire keeps the creatures at bay. Because they belong to the night, they fear its light. If the fire should go out, we would be at their mercy, for then we would be in their element. They can see in the darkness."

"What sort of creatures are they?" Grant found himself glancing around uneasily at the darkness just beyond the ring of light.

"I know not, for none have faced their wrath and lived to tell of it. But it's whispered that they're cruel, dangerous beasts who thrive on the blood of their prey.''

He studied the meager supply of sticks and branches that Kylia had hauled from the surrounding brush. "As soon as I've eaten, I'll gather more wood."

She nodded. "But remember to stay within the circle of firelight. You mustn't risk leaving its protection."

In the distance they heard a scream that might have been animal or human. The sound of it scraped over their nerves.

Grant felt a chill race along his spine and wondered at it. Like all warriors, he'd known fear a time or two on the field of battle. But at least there he knew something about his opponents, for even barbarians from far-flung regions fought with sword and knife and arrow. Beasts that inhabited the Forest of Darkness would be a dangerous foe unlike anything he'd ever encountered. He had no desire to test his skill against such adversaries.

"Step back, my lady."

Grant used the blade of his sword to hack at

the gnarled branches of a tree. Sweat beaded his forehead as he and Kylia dragged the limbs across the campsite.

"Until now I hadn't realized how small was the circle of light cast by the fire. No wonder you were able to find so little wood."

"Aye." She wiped her hands down her skirt. "I've nearly swept the ground clean to keep the fire going."

"This should give us some time." He tossed the branches on the fire and watched as the flames leaped high in the air, before dropping weakly to the ground.

At once Kylia was beside him. "What is it, my lord?"

"I'd hoped to take leave of this place." He shook his head to clear it. The weakness caught him by surprise. "But here I am, feeling as helpless as a bairn."

She gave him a gentle smile. "You were, whether you care to admit it or not, gravely wounded. It will take time to regain your strength."

"Time." He spat the word. "We haven't the time to waste here in this place. I'm needed in my fortress."

"Rest now." Kylia shook the grass from her traveling cloak and draped it around him. "Soon enough we'll be gone from here."

Within minutes Grant was fast asleep.

As Kylia drew near the fire for warmth, she heard the rustling sounds just beyond the circle of light, and knew the forest creatures were watching. She glanced at the pile of firewood and shivered. Here in the Forest of Darkness there was neither day nor night. Only eternal darkness.

How soon, she wondered, before the firewood was gone?

Then would they have to face the mythical beasts that no man had ever lived to describe.

Chapter Six

Kylia fed wood to the fire and watched the flames leap, sending shadows dancing across the campsite. When Grant moaned in his sleep she hurried to kneel beside him, touching a hand to his forehead. He flinched and she realized with a shock that the fever was back. His flesh was hot to the touch. What's more, his pain had not subsided. She could feel it, pulsing through him in waves. Her fault, she thought with a twinge of guilt. She'd known, of course, that some wounds needed much more care than others, yet she'd allowed herself to get distracted by the mundane chores of this strange new world.

Oh, if only Allegra were here. She was so much better at healing, Kylia thought.

She placed her hands on either side of Grant's head and began to chant the ancient words that would drive the evil from his body.

Hours later, her voice hoarse, her arms throbbing from the effort to keep them outstretched, she allowed herself the luxury of sitting back on her heels, pressing a hand to the small of her back. She would ease her discomfort for only a moment, she promised herself as her lids closed and her head bobbed. Seconds later she jerked awake and struggled to focus on the firelight, but her eyes swam from the effort and she allowed the lids to flutter, then close.

She would soon have to add more branches to the fire.

It was her last coherent thought before the need for sleep dragged her down.

Kylia awoke with a start at the strange rustling sounds. Confused, disoriented, she sat up rubbing her eyes. Beside her, Grant stirred, then stared in disbelief at the shadowy figures creeping from their places of concealment in the nearby forest.

"The fire," he shouted.

Kylia gave a hiss of self-disgust. She'd fallen asleep and allowed the fire to burn out. All that remained were gleaming coals, giving off enough light to see the outlines of the fearsome creatures. Some were foaming at the mouth, others snarling, fangs bared, as they started forward.

"Take this." Grant pressed his dirk into her hand.

She was already shaking her head. "I couldn't harm any creature."

"It may be your only chance," he whispered as he got to his feet, brandishing his sword. "For I've no doubt they mean us harm."

As the last of the fire died, the night was suddenly alive with creatures, some with hair bristling, others standing upright, as tall as trees. One great shaggy beast rushed forward, and Kylia stared in horrified fascination at its two heads.

"Get behind me." Grant stepped in front of her, holding his sword aloft.

The creature's two vicious jaws opened, revealing razor-sharp fangs. Two pair of gleaming red eyes were fixed on Grant with a look meant to freeze the blood in his veins.

Just then a snake more than six feet in length slithered from the forest and began weaving its way toward them. Its body was the thickness of a great hollow log, proving it would have no trouble swallowing them whole.

Joining it were more than a dozen creatures larger than a horse, some snarling, others silent as they formed an uneven ring around the two intruders.

"Now I know why my fellow Highland warriors fear this place." Grant drew an arm around Kylia, offering her what little comfort he could. "I'll fight to my last breath, my lady. My only regret is that I'll not be able to save you, for I know my strength is no match for these creatures."

He peered through the gloom. As darkness closed in around them, the forest seemed alive with every manner of beast imaginable. "These are the creatures of my worst nightmare." He pointed with his sword at the two-headed monster creeping closer. "As a child, I used to see the likes of him in the twisted shapes and shadows of the night. I even had a name for the creature. *Dubh gall.*"

"Dark stranger?"

Grant shot her a look. "Is that what it means?"

"Aye." She nodded. "You didn't recognize the ancient words?"

He shook his head, keeping his gaze fixed on the monster. "The name came to me only in my sleep. Until now."

Kylia nodded toward the giant snake. "Such a creature was always present in my childhood dreams whenever they were troubled. When I described it to my mum, she told me there were no snakes in our kingdom, but such creatures did exist beyond our shores."

"That's true. Though I've never seen one as big as that." Seeing the two-headed beast creeping closer, Grant slashed out with his sword, forcing the creature back. "But such a beast as that one exists nowhere else in our land except here."

As the circle of light grew smaller and dimmer, more and more creatures crept from their places of concealment, until the forest became a bloodcurdling chorus of high-pitched cries, savage howls and teeth-baring snarls.

Grant turned to face the worst of the creatures. "Stand with your back to mine, my lady."

Kylia did as he ordered, and swallowed back the fear that threatened to paralyze her.

"Hold your dirk firmly, blade pointed out and slightly upward, so that the creatures know you mean them harm."

She followed his example, though her heart was drumming so painfully in her chest, she thought he could surely hear.

"Within minutes the last of the coals will burn out, leaving us in complete darkness. When that happens, the beasts will attack."

"If that be true, how can we defend ourselves?"

"We'll see their eyes. It will give us something to aim for."

"Grant." She knew her voice was trembling. It couldn't be helped. "I would give anything to save you from this place. But I can't find it in my heart to harm even these creatures."

He muttered an oath before turning his head slightly, so that she could feel the warmth of his breath on her cheek. "Forgive me for even asking it, my lady, for I've witnessed your tender heart. As for me, I intend to fight to the death. When the battle begins, I beg you to run to where my steed is tied and flee this place of horrors.''

She shook her head. ''I won't leave you, my lord.''

''You must. Don't you see?'' He turned his back on the approaching danger and closed his hands on her upper arms in a painful grasp. ''I don't mind losing my life. But I'd die a happy man knowing my life was spent saving yours. Now promise me you'll flee.''

Already his face was beginning to blur, and she knew the last of the coals were growing cool. ''Please don't spend our last moments on earth like this, my lord. I'll not leave you, for I was destined to be with you. Whether in this life or the next, it matters not to me. My place is here with you. Nothing you can say or do will drive me away.''

He drew her close for one quick kiss, the merest brush of mouth to mouth, while the chorus of chilling sounds filled the forest.

''Oh, my lady. My beautiful Kylia. If only

there had been time to show you my land. My people. My life.''

''I regret that more than you can know. I had truly hoped to learn the name of the one who betrayed you.''

''At a time like this, it seems less important than the fact that we must bid farewell in this dark forest before we even have time to know each other.''

She stared into his eyes and smiled. ''It's true that you know me not. But I know you, my lord. I've known you all my life.''

Her words stirred him. ''Farewell, my lady.'' He kissed her again, this time lingering over her lips. Despite the chill of the dark forest, he felt the quick rush of heat and was warmed by it.

The last spark created a burst of fiery light, blinding them before it burned out, plunging them into total darkness. Suddenly they were surrounded by gleaming feral eyes.

Grant lashed out, but his blade cut cleanly through the air, touching nothing. Keeping one arm around Kylia, he thrust his sword into the darkness. Again he felt nothing but air.

''Where are you?'' he demanded of the creatures. "I can hear you breathe, can see your eyes burning in the darkness. Come closer, cowards."

Again he parried, but his sword sang through the air, touching nothing.

Kylia felt something at the hem of her gown and let out a scream as she imagined the snake slithering around her ankles.

"Are you hurt?" Grant demanded.

"Nay." She struggled for breath, then said louder, "Nay. Like my dreams, I thought..."

At her sudden silence he drew her close. "What is it, my lady? You've been harmed, haven't you?"

"Nay. But something just occurred to me."

He glanced around, feeling his skin crawl as the feral red eyes drew closer, until the night was alive with them. "What is it, Kylia?"

"The Forest of Darkness. The creatures. I don't believe they exist, except in our minds."

"What are you saying?" He pointed with the tip of his sword. "Look around you. They're everywhere. We can both see them."

"Aye." She put a hand to still the pounding of her heart. "But I see my worst fear. A snake.

You see the two-headed creature of your nightmares. And when the fire burns brightly, neither of us sees anything."

He digested this while all around him the forest was filled with chilling sounds. Suddenly he caught her hand. "If you're right in this, we can walk freely across the clearing and toss a fresh log on the coals."

"Aye."

"If you're wrong, we'll never feel the warmth of a fire again."

Her hand trembled in his. "Then we'll die together, my lord."

"You're willing to risk it?"

"I am."

He drew her close and wrapped an arm around her shoulders. Together they took a step, and then another. Though the snarls and cries intensified, causing them to halt in panic, neither of them felt a sting of pain.

"Stay with me, Kylia." Grant took another step and began feeling around in the dark for the pile of branches. When at last he touched them, he stooped and gathered an armload. Then he moved closer until he could feel the warmth of the coals. Seconds after dropping the wood, a tiny flicker of flame appeared along one thin branch. A few moments later the flame grew, until it hissed and snapped, creating a blaze of firelight that pierced the darkness.

Grant looked around. There was no trace of the creatures that had tormented them. The night had grown ominously silent. And though he could see, just beyond the circle of light, what appeared to be red eyes watching from the cover of darkness, they remained hidden in shadow.

He drew Kylia close and pressed his lips to a tangle of hair at her temple. "My beautiful, clever Kylia. What would have happened to us if you hadn't uncovered the mystery of this place?"

"We would have remained paralyzed by our fears, my lord. And unable to return to your land." She pushed a little away and looked into his eyes. "And now, while the fire holds those fears at bay, we must leave this place. Are you strong enough to ride?"

"Aye. Now that I've been spared a duel with monsters, I feel strong enough to tackle an entire army." He bent and retrieved her traveling cloak, tenderly wrapping it around her. "I'll fetch my horse."

As he walked away, Kylia watched him and wondered at the strange stirrings deep inside. Each time he touched her, kissed her, the feelings grew and deepened.

Was this love? Or was this merely a desire to mate, as she'd seen in other creatures?

She wanted it to be more than that. She wanted to know everything about this man who so touched her heart. What he'd been like as a child. How he'd been chosen as laird over all other men.

She was eager to see his land. To meet his people. For she had no doubt he was the one she'd been fated to meet.

Of course, it might take her some time to convince him of that fact. But now that they'd solved the mystery of the Forest of Darkness, they had been given the gift of time.

Time.

She smiled as he led his steed toward her and helped her into the saddle before pulling himself up behind her. She leaned back, loving the way his arms wrapped around her as he took the reins.

Though they traversed the forest for hours, they saw no more monsters. Now that they'd conquered their fear, they were free of the darkness that had held them in its grip.

When at last they left the Forest of Darkness behind, they found themselves in a Highland meadow, abloom with heather, bathed in dazzling sunlight.

Chapter Seven

"Oh." Kylia gave a sigh as she looked around. "This is every bit as lovely as the Mystical Kingdom. Is this your home?"

"Nay." Grant slowed his mount to allow her to enjoy the beauty. "We have another day's ride before we reach my fortress. But the countryside is much like this. There are meadows surrounded by glorious mountains, the peaks wreathed in clouds. And running through the land is a loch so clear you can see to the very bottom."

She could hear the warmth in his tone. "It would seem you're missing your land and your people, my lord."

"Aye. I only hope they're missing me, as well."

She turned to glance at him over her shoulder. "And why wouldn't they miss their laird?"

"I've failed them. Failed to protect them from harm. Failed to protect them in war by leading my warriors into a trap, causing them pain and humiliation. They have a right to doubt their leader."

"You couldn't know you were being betrayed by someone you trusted. Soon enough they'll know the truth."

"I pray it is as you say, my lady. For all I know they may have already called a council to declare another leader in my stead."

As they came up over a rise they caught sight of a flock of sheep grazing in the meadow. Several figures could be seen moving among the animals.

Grant veered off the path he'd been following, urging his horse into a thick stand of trees. He slid to the ground and reached up to lift Kylia down.

"Stay here." His voice held a hint of steel as he pulled himself into the saddle.

Surprised, Kylia stared at him in bewilderment. "Where are you going?"

"To stop those thieves from stealing sheep."

She caught his arm. "How do you know they're thieves? Perhaps they live in that cottage across the meadow."

He pointed to the plume of dark smoke curling above a thatched roof, forming a haze on the horizon. "Peasants and sheepherders don't burn their own cottages, my lady. That can only be the work of villains."

"They've set fire to the cottage? I'd thought it nothing more than a cooking fire." Before she could say more, he took off with a thunder of hoofbeats.

Kylia stared after him in amazement. He'd had only a few precious moments to assess the situation, but he'd moved with all speed to help people he didn't even know.

Though he'd cautioned her to remain here, she ignored his words. She bent down to retrieve a broken tree limb, thinking to help. As she straightened, she was yanked backward, causing the stick to slip from her grasp. Before she could utter a sound she was lifted off her feet and tossed roughly over a man's shoulder. Though she kicked and pummeled him with her fists, he ignored her feeble protests as he raced across the meadow to join his comrades.

Just as suddenly, she was set on her feet. An arm came around her, holding her firmly, while the edge of a knife was pressed to her throat.

Her captor shouted at Grant, "The woman dies unless you lower your weapon at once."

Kylia was horrified to see Grant do as the man commanded. The moment he lowered his sword, the band of thieves set upon him, attacking with knives and fists. All she could do was watch with a feeling of sick dread as he was knocked to the ground.

She heard a low rumble of laughter from the man behind her. The sound of it had her trembling with a feeling she'd never known before. Anger. A terrible anger at the injustice of it. The feeling had her blood running cold.

She closed her eyes and began to chant. Softly at first, then growing louder as the anger built, becoming a slow, simmering rage.

The hands holding her seemed to lose their strength. Her captor let out a gasp of surprise as he dropped weakly to his knees in the grass. All he could do was watch helplessly as Kylia turned on him, arms outstretched, and continued chanting words he'd never heard before.

Grant's attackers let out a roar of laughter at the sight of her.

One of them shouted, "She holds her arms like swords, thinking to frighten us."

"Aye," another jeered. "And spouts foolish words that have no meaning. Get up, you fool," he shouted to his comrade. "Why are you leaving us with all the work?"

Their laughter died in their throats when their weapons slipped from their fingers as though tugged by invisible strings, landing on the ground at their feet. Before they could move, Grant bent and retrieved his own weapon. Then he paused to touch a hand to Kylia's cheek. Just a touch, but she felt the warmth of it through her veins and found the words of her chant dying in her throat.

The thieves used that moment of silence to flee, leaving behind the flock of sheep, and the menacing man and woman. Even the one who'd threatened her was on his feet and racing to the safety of the surrounding forest.

One of the thieves caught a bleating lamb and tossed it about his neck before disappearing with his comrades into the trees on the far side of the meadow.

Grant gave her a look of concern. "Are you truly unharmed, my lady?"

"Aye. Don't worry about me. Go after them, my lord."

Instead of doing as she urged, he raced toward the burning cottage. Just as he disappeared inside, the roof collapsed inward.

"No!" With a shout she began running after him.

By the time she reached the cottage, the fire was so intense it was impossible to see past the wall of flame. Twice she tried to dart into the fire, only to be driven back. In desperation she drew her cloak firmly around her head and face until all but her eyes were covered. Then she forced her way past the falling timbers into the very heart of the blaze, where Grant was holding the body of a man in his arms. Behind him was a woman holding an infant, while a terrified toddler clung to her skirts.

Seeing Kylia, Grant shouted, "Lead them out of here. Quickly, for the last of the timbers will soon collapse."

Ignoring the fire that licked along her skirts, Kylia draped her cloak around the woman's shoulders before scooping up the child. When she realized that the woman was too terrified to move, she caught her hand and dragged her along, step by slow, painful step, until they had escaped the wall of flame. They dropped to their knees, choking and gasping for air.

There was a great roar as the cottage exploded, the walls collapsing inward, sending flames shooting high in the air. For the space of a heartbeat Kylia watched in horror, knowing no one could survive such a thing. A feeling of immense sadness stole over her. She'd saved strangers, but couldn't save the man whose image had been with her since childhood.

As the flames and smoke billowed skyward, she caught sight of two figures lying in the grass on the far side of the cottage. With a cry she stumbled toward them and dropped to her knees beside Grant.

His skin was black from soot and ash. His clothes still smoldered as he coughed and struggled for breath.

"Praise heaven you're alive." Kylia touched a hand to his cheek.

Between coughs he managed to whisper, "See to him."

The stranger's arms were badly burned, as was his face. What worried Kylia more than his burns were the wounds to his neck and chest, bleeding profusely.

As she began stripping away his tunic, the woman approached and fell to the grass weeping. "Oh, my beloved Ewald. Please don't leave me."

Kylia touched a hand to her sleeve. "Not all these wounds were caused by the fire."

The woman shook her head. "The thieves forced their way into our cottage. While I did my best to protect the wee ones, Ewald defended himself with nothing but his fists. Those monsters left him to die, then set fire to the roof before turning to our flock."

At her husband's moan, she turned pleading eyes to Kylia. "Please, my lady. Can you ease his pain?"

Kylia felt a wave of frustration at her inadequacy. If only Allegra were here. Her older sister would know exactly what to do. She was about to explain that she knew little about healing burns when she caught sight of the child's tears. They touched her as nothing else could. This was no time to be faint of heart.

She gave a sigh. "I'll do what I can. I'll need water."

At once the woman dashed toward a nearby stream, returning with a brimming bucket.

After bathing the stranger's wounds, Kylia soaked a cloth in the water and lay it over his charred flesh.

The woman carried a blackened jug from the smoldering ruins and set it beside Kylia. At her questioning look the woman explained, "Spirits, my lady. My man rarely drank, so the jug is full. You might use this to cleanse his wounds."

"Aye." Kylia poured a liberal amount of whiskey over the wounds, and proceeded to bind them. When she had finished, she wrapped him in her traveling cloak.

She looked up to see Grant returning from the stream, where he'd bathed his burned flesh. Though she could read the pain in his eyes, he made no mention of it as he began cleaning several fish he'd caught.

When the meal was ready he passed it around, seeing that the woman and her children ate their fill.

As if in a trance the woman ate, all the while staring at her sleeping husband. "What will we do if the thieves return?"

Grant knelt beside her. "Have you no clan? No family or friends nearby?"

She shook her head. "Our families live in the village. We came to this far meadow because it seemed a fine place to raise our family and tend our herds. But now that the thieves know we are helpless, they'll wait until you leave and attack again. Next time, they'll see we are dead so they can steal the entire flock."

Grant knew the truth of her statement. Though it grieved him to put off his return to his own home, for he was anxious about the safety of his people, he couldn't leave this family alone and helpless.

He patted her hand and glanced over at Kylia. "The lady and I will stay until your man is strong enough to travel. If you desire, we'll accompany you to your village, where there will be family and friends to tend to your needs."

The woman closed her eyes while giving a sigh of relief. "I thank you, my lord." She turned. "And you, my lady." She cuddled her infant in one arm and drew her toddler to her before looking around in alarm. "Alas, I can't even offer you shelter from the night."

"We need nothing but this fire. I'll keep watch while you and the wee ones sleep. On the morrow, I'll set about finding some way to make your journey back to your clan possible." Grant gave her a gentle smile. "My name is Grant, laird of the clan MacCallum. The lady is Kylia, of the clan Drummond."

"I am Flora. And these are our children, Ian and Donald. We are of the clan Kerr." She drew close to the sleeping man and lay down in the grass, gathering her children to her bosom. Ex-

hausted by their ordeal, they soon joined him in
sleep.

Kylia got to her feet and hurried toward
Grant, who was already striding toward the
woods. "What can I do to help?"

He paused and turned. In his eyes was a look
that warmed her more than any touch. "You've
already done so much, my lady. Your courage
leaves me without words."

She shook her head, sending dark curls dancing. "It was your courage that saved these people, my lord."

"Nay. It was nothing compared with what
you did." He reached up to tuck a stray curl
behind her ear.

At once she felt the rush of heat and wondered that her heart didn't leap clear out of her
chest.

He kept his hand there a moment longer, loving the look of softness that came into her eyes.
He found himself enjoying the quick rush of
heat, and the slow, steady throbbing in his loins.
After the ordeal they'd been through, touching
her was a reward, like coming home.

She could feel the change in him. A tension

that conveyed itself to her, as well. As she started to pull back he closed a hand on her shoulder.

"I must kiss you, my lady."

"This is hardly the place…"

Her words were cut off abruptly as he dragged her into his arms, crushing her against his chest. His mouth covered hers in a kiss so hot, so filled with hunger, it unleashed a matching hunger inside her.

His was such a clever, agile mouth. Strong, firm lips. A tongue that dueled with hers. The taste of him, so potently male, had her head spinning, her heart racing. The blood in her veins seemed to ebb and flow, causing the ground beneath her feet to shift and tilt until she was forced to grasp his waist to keep from falling.

"My lord. Wait." She pushed away, struggling for air. "I can't think when you kiss me."

His smile was quick and dangerous. "That's exactly what I had in mind, my lady." He drew her close and ran soft, nibbling kisses along her temple, down her cheek, to the tip of her nose.

''There's no need to think when we can feel such as this.''

The sweetness of it had her relaxing in his arms until he took the kiss deeper. There it was again. That little jolt to the heart, and then the warmth sliding through her veins, leaving her sighing with desire.

This time it was Kylia who reached for him, her arms encircling his neck, her body straining toward his. With her mouth on his she poured herself into the kiss, feeling the heat, the excitement, the flutter of danger.

Her body felt so alive. As though with one touch, he'd opened her up to all that was new and possible. She was, she realized, already wildly in love with this man. She wanted to tell him. To shout it out for the whole world to hear. What's more, she wanted desperately to show him. And she did, by returning his kisses with a fervor that had them both gasping.

''How soon,'' she whispered against his lips, ''before we leave for your home?''

The sweetness of her breath mingled with his. He breathed her in, wanting more than anything in the world to taste more. To take more than her kisses. He wanted her with a fierceness that was like an ache.

He dipped his head and kissed her again, while his hands moved over her, pleasuring them both. With each touch, each kiss, the fire within them grew. The need within them churned, until they were half-mad with desire.

Cautioning himself to go slowly, Grant drew back. "I know you'd like the comfort of my home, my lady. I know I've already asked much of you, but I would beg another favor."

She leaned close, hoping he might taste of her lips again. Now that she'd experienced the heat, she wanted more. So much more. If he asked, she would give all. Here and now, in the grass beside the stream, under the cover of darkness. "There is no need to beg, my lord. You need but ask and it is done."

He took another step back, alarmed at the fire that flamed between them. He felt so seduced by her beauty, he could burn to ash with a simple touch.

Knowing he could have what he wanted only made him more aware than ever of the need to protect her from herself.

"I hope you won't mind tarrying here until these good people are safe."

She looked down, knowing he'd be able to read the disappointment in her eyes. Not that she minded staying in this humble meadow. But at the moment, her only thought was to have him kiss her again and again, until the heat became an inferno. Did he not feel what she felt?

Her words were abrupt. "As you wish, my lord."

"Thank you, my lady." He brought her hands to his lips, pressing a kiss to each palm. Then, before temptation could take over his resolve, he turned resolutely away.

As he made his way in the darkness he clenched his hands into fists. They were, he realized, shaking.

A short time later Grant returned, his arms laden with logs. He was relieved to see Kylia asleep with the others.

Throughout the long night, while he tended the fire and kept watch over the flock, he found himself studying the way she looked by firelight. So sweet. So beautiful, she took his breath away.

Whenever he got too close to her, he forgot that she wasn't like other women. It was becoming more and more difficult to step away from the invitation he could read in those eyes. But it was necessary to remember that he was a mere man, while she was a witch.

A witch. There, he'd admitted it.

It was the first time he'd allowed himself to think such a thing. But he'd seen the way she could control men's minds. With nothing more than a lifting of her arms, and a few ancient words chanted in that melodic voice of hers, she could stop an army of barbarians.

It was one thing to control men's minds, and quite another to lose control of her own. When she'd offered to accompany him to his Highland fortress, he'd accepted her generosity without a thought to what it might cost her. It hadn't occurred to him that this was a woman who had never before confronted evil. But twice now he'd seen the fear and confusion in her eyes. Had witnessed the pain that his world could bring to her.

He clenched his fists, fighting a wave of guilt.

There was something else he could read in her eyes. The glorious awakening of desire.

It was bad enough that he'd asked her to use her powers to save his wretched hide. He'd be damned if he'd take advantage of her innocence for his own pleasure.

Still, the temptation was almost more than he could resist.

He would have to remain vigilant to see that he returned her to her home as he'd found her. Sweet, untouched and unsullied by his own all-too-human desires.

Chapter Eight

In the heat of the afternoon Flora lay the sleeping infant beside Ewald, who was also asleep. She glanced at Grant, naked to the waist, busily repairing a wooden cart that had been damaged in the fire. "The laird of the MacCallum clan is a good man," she said to Kylia. "There aren't many men who would give such care to strangers."

"Aye. A good man." Kylia couldn't seem to look away from the play of muscles that bunched and tensed across his back and shoulders with every movement.

She'd dreamed of him last night. Holding her. Kissing her. The images had been so real, she'd awakened with a start only to see the object of her thoughts keeping a lonely vigil across the meadow, near the flock of sheep.

What was she to do about these feelings? There were times when she thought she just had to touch him, to assure herself that he was real. After a lifetime of seeing his face in her mind, she feared he might disappear before she had a chance to tell him just what was in her heart.

What was in her heart?

She wasn't certain if what she was feeling was true love, but she cared deeply about him. And with every day spent in his company, those feelings grew.

"Is the laird taking you to his home to be his wife?"

Flora's words broke through Kylia's reverie. She looked over in surprise. "Nay. I accompany him because he needs my help."

"How can you help such a great laird?"

Kylia's cheeks felt warm. What could she possibly say to this woman that would make sense? "I have certain gifts which the laird has need of."

"Gifts, my lady?"

Kylia's flush deepened. "I can see things."

"What things do you see?"

"The past. Occasionally the future. It comes to me in visions." She waited, afraid to breathe, for fear of this young woman's reaction. Instead of the rejection she anticipated, the young woman accepted her explanation without question.

Flora's mouth was split by a wide smile. "Oh, my lady, my grandmother was also thus blessed. She told me, when she first met Ewald, that he would ask for my hand. Though I didn't believe her at first, I was later persuaded just how wise a woman she was. Our family always knew that she had special gifts which the rest of us didn't possess." She looked down, avoiding Kylia's eyes. "Since you're blessed, could you tell me..." Embarrassed, she swallowed back her words.

Kylia reached a hand to hers. "You needn't ask. I can read the question in your heart. This will be the daughter you desire."

The young woman gave a soft laugh. "Not even Ewald knows about it yet. I wasn't even certain myself."

"Believe it," Kylia said gently, touching a

hand to the young woman's abdomen. "She will be a beautiful child, and will bring you much happiness in your old age."

"Thank you, my lady." Flora clasped her hands together.

As Kylia got to her feet and started toward Grant, she caught a glimpse of the young woman wiping a tear of joy from her eye and was forced to whisper a word of thanks to the Fates that had given her this strange gift of sight. Though such a thing set her apart from many, it was as much a part of her as the color of her eyes, or the texture of her hair. And not something she would ever care to deny. Though her family had been forced into exile because of their extraordinary gifts, Kylia wouldn't change a thing even if she could.

While Grant readied the cart for a journey to the distant village, Kylia took comfort in the water of the bubbling stream. It had always been her refuge and her greatest pleasure. Even here, so far from home, she felt connected as she stepped into the clear, cold water. As she splashed deeper she spied the fat salmon lurking in the shelter of submerged rocks. It took her less than a minute to snatch the fish from its lair and toss it onto shore. While she made several leisurely turns across the stream she caught sight of more salmon. By the time she walked from the water and hurriedly dressed, she was able to fill her skirts with enough salmon to feed them all.

At the campsite Ewald lay talking softly with his wife. It was clear that he was in a great deal of pain, but he managed a smile as Kylia approached.

"My lady. Flora tells me that I owe you my life."

"Nay, sir. If it hadn't been for Lord Mac-Callum's quick thinking, neither of you would have survived the fire. All I did was try to ease a bit of your suffering." She knelt down and showed them her catch. "With such as this we'll dine like royalty tonight."

"Let me help." Flora knelt beside her and the two young women began scaling the fish before setting them to cook over the hot coals.

From the ruins of the cottage Flora retrieved the remains of flour and sugar stored in a small dirt cellar. Soon the air was redolent with the fragrance of biscuits baking.

By the time Grant laid down his tools and joined them, their mouths were watering.

Though the fare was simple, they sat around the fire, savoring the food, and the chance to finally relax in one another's company. Soon the children were asleep, tucked into the folds of Kylia's cloak. Grant and Ewald shared sips from the jug of spirits, while Kylia and Flora drank strong tea and chatted softly as darkness gathered over the land.

Later, as Kylia drifted off to sleep beside the fire, she saw Grant take up his vigil near the flock. Though she longed to join him, she was forced to give in to her weariness. She slept in the knowledge that he would keep watch through the night, and see to their safety. There was such comfort in the fact that this strong man was watching out for all of them.

At first light Grant hitched his horse to the cart before helping Ewald and the children into the back, which was lined with Kylia's cloak. Then he helped Flora up to the hard seat and handed her the reins.

As the horse and cart started forward, Grant and Kylia urged the flock to follow, while they walked slowly behind, keeping an eye out for any stragglers.

The journey took the better part of a day, and they reached the village of the clan Kerr shortly before dusk. Long before they arrived, men on horseback had spotted them. While some remained to accompany them, others raced ahead to carry word to their families that they were on their way. By the time they arrived, the entire village had assembled on the green to greet them with a feast.

And what a feast. There were platters of mutton and fish, as well as a whole roasted stag. There were tarts and biscuits, and scones heavy with currants and berries. There were hundreds of questions, and warm embraces from the young couple's family, as Grant and Kylia were warmly thanked for saving their lives and returning them safely to their village.

Through it all Grant and Kylia smiled and acknowledged their words with as much grace as they could manage. But soon the heat and the food and the knowledge that they were finally safe had their eyes heavy and their heads bobbing.

With much ceremony they were escorted to the finest hut in the village and taken to separate sleeping chambers, where they were helped out of their filthy clothes and into warm baths before being offered beds of softest fur.

The women of the village vied for the honor of washing their clothes and preparing them for the morrow's journey. But while the women chatted, and the men drank their spirits and spoke in whispers about the beautiful young woman and great laird who had rescued one of their own, Grant and Kylia were oblivious to all but the sweet dreams that played through their minds as they slept.

"How can I ever thank you, my lady?" As the entire village gathered to bid goodbye to their visitors, Flora stepped forward to catch Kylia's hand and lift it to her lips. "Without your kindness, we would have surely perished at the hands of the barbarians."

"I require no thanks, Flora." Refreshed from her night of sleep, restored by the luxury of a bath and fine food, Kylia embraced her new friend. Her clothes, and even her hair smelled of rainwater and evergreen. Her smile was as bright as the sun. "I rejoice that you and your family are now safely home with your clan."

"That is my wish for you, as well, my lady. May you soon be safely home with those who love you."

Klyia thought about the sweet paradise she called home, and realized with a pang just how much she missed it. Though she had willingly undertaken this journey, her beloved Mystical Kingdom was never far from her thoughts.

She accepted the hooded cloak from one of the women and tossed it over her shoulders before being helped into the saddle of Grant's steed. After taking leave of all the men who stood in a circle, Grant pulled himself up behind her and caught up the reins.

"Watch your back," Ewald called, offering his hand in friendship. "The barbarians may come seeking revenge."

"I'll take care. Now I must return to my own people, for I've been away from them too long." Amid calls from the villagers, Grant flicked the reins and the horse took off with a flurry of hoofbeats.

As they left the village behind, Grant couldn't resist pressing his face to Kylia's hair. It felt so good to be holding her again. To be breathing in the soft, womanly scent of her that had become such an important part of him on this journey.

She turned her head slightly and found his lips brushing her temple. It was a jolt to her system.

"How far to your home, my lord?"

"Another day." His voice lowered with feeling. "Another night." The thought of spending another night alone with her had his blood heating.

Kylia felt the skitter along her spine and wondered, as she did so often, whether he felt such things, too. Or was it different for a man? Especially one as worldly as Grant.

She glanced at his face, but could read nothing in his eyes. She turned her face to the wind and breathed deeply, filling her lungs.

"Tell me about your home and family, my lord, for I'm eager to know all I can about them."

"I don't recall my father or mother, since both died before my second year of life. But

I've been told that my father was a great warrior. His name is still spoken with awe among our kinsmen. It's said he was fearless in battle, and a fearsome foe to those who crossed him. Still, he was a fair man, and a kind one, who opened his home to widows and orphans.''

"You mentioned an aunt who lives with you."

He nodded. "Hazlet, my father's sister. She was betrothed to his trusted friend, Ranald. When both men died on the field of battle, she was filled with grief, and took to her chambers. But when Hazlet learned that my mother's grief had brought the birth pains too soon, she went to my mother's room and stayed with her—" his tone softened, and Kylia could hear the warmth of affection in it "—until she was safely delivered of my brother, Dougal."

"You love him very much."

"Aye. How could I not? He and I have spent every waking hour together since the day he was born."

She nodded in understanding, for it had been the same with her and her sisters. "And your aunt? Did she never marry?"

"Hazlet's love and grief were such that she

would never permit another man to win her heart. She was nurse to Dougal, and trusted advisor to us both as we grew to manhood."

"She must be very proud that you have been elevated to laird of your clan, as your father before you."

He was silent for long moments before saying, "Perhaps, by the time I return, I will no longer be laird. The council of elders has the power to bestow the title on another in my stead."

"Would they do that without giving you the opportunity to speak in your own defense?"

"I know not. But this I know. I would rather die than bring dishonor to my father's name."

Kylia fell silent, for she understood the depth of his pain. The love she felt for her family was so great she would gladly face death over dishonor.

It was, she realized, one more reason why this man had begun to mean so much to her. They shared not only a love for family, but also a fierce desire to do the right thing, the honorable thing, for the sake of those who loved them.

Chapter Nine

"Look, my lady."

They had been climbing steadily all day. Now, as they crested yet another hill and looked out over a Highland meadow, the sun was obscured behind a distant mountain peak. Fingers of mauve and orchid and deep purple slanted across the land, casting long shadows from gnarled trees and tumbled rocks.

"Amazing." Kylia's voice was whispered, in deference to the majesty of the scene spread out before her. "There's such a wild, primitive look to it."

"Aye. And always it stirs my heart." Grant brought his mount to a halt and sat for long moments, drinking in the scene.

At last he slid from the animal's back before reaching up to her. He lifted her from the saddle and she felt the quick sizzle of excitement along her spine as his arms came around her. When he set her on her feet, she stood perfectly still, breathing deeply to clear her mind.

He tethered the horse and removed the blanket roll from behind the saddle. "I'll get a fire going, my lady, and then see about finding something to eat."

While he built a fire, Kylia forced herself to move. Needing something to do, she unrolled the fur throw, intending to shake it before spreading it on the grass. She looked down in surprise at the sight of several bundles inside. Unwrapping them, she let out a laugh of delight.

"You've no need to hunt our food, my lord. It seems the villagers are still showing their gratitude, even though we've left them far behind." She held up the first bundle. "Dried mutton. Enough for many nights. And in this…" She unrolled a second to reveal sugared scones. "They wanted to make certain we didn't starve before arriving at your fortress."

"Such good people. They didn't need to do this."

"They wanted to show how much they love you for saving one of their own."

He stepped back from the fire, brushing his hands along his tunic. "They love you as well, my lady." The look he gave her was so hot, so fierce, it had her heart faltering. He touched a finger to her cheek. "How could they not?"

That simple touch had her paralyzed. She forgot to breathe. Her heart forgot to beat as he stared down into her eyes.

She wanted him to kiss her. Wanted it desperately.

He seemed to consider it, before he abruptly turned away and removed the flask at his waist. Over his shoulder, he called, "I'll fetch water from the stream while you uncover the rest of our meal."

She watched him walk away and waited for her heart to settle. As she began unwrapping the food, she pondered how she could possibly deal with these strange, new emotions that battered her. For so long she had lived a simple life in a calm environment. Now she'd been thrust into a world of violent, explosive emotions that had her feeling confused, troubled, throwing her completely off balance.

She sat back on her heels and closed her eyes, picturing in her mind her family gathered around the table. The image had her smiling.

"Oh, Gram. Mum. You both lived in this world before you returned to the Mystical Kingdom. You've experienced all these things. I need your wisdom now." She lifted her head to the night sky and had to laugh at the clouds that looked exactly like Jeremy astride her winged horse Moonlight. There was his round little face, looking so serious. His little waistcoat flapping in the breeze. Another cloud rolled past, and she gasped as she recognized old Bessie, stooped over a kettle, stirring something. She could see clearly the apron tied around her thick middle, and the big wooden paddle she always used while cooking.

These cloud formations were no accident. Kylia knew at once they'd been sent by her family to comfort her. She watched Jeremy drift higher and higher, until he seemed to touch the stars, followed by Bessie, who lifted her wooden paddle to wave.

Kylia sighed. Both troll and hunchback had been mistreated in this world. But both had forgiven their tormentors, and spoke fondly of the many good people they had known. People who had given them aid and comfort and shelter in their time of need.

By the time Grant returned from the stream, Kylia was kneeling on the fur, a dreamy smile playing on her lips.

"You look happy, my lady."

"Aye." She watched as he reclined on the opposite side of the fur and began to eat. "I realize that, despite the violence in your land, there is much to like, as well. There is such kindness in your people."

He broke open a scone and popped it into his mouth. "Not to mention some excellent cooks."

Kylia laughed. "Aye. There is that. Tell me about the cook at your fortress."

"Her name is Mester. She cooked for my father and his father before him. And she has cooked for my brother and me since we were born."

"Such a long time."

"Aye. And in all that time I've never known her to cook something I didn't like."

"You must be easy to please."

"Or perhaps she is as gifted as you, my lady, and can see in my heart what I like before I tell her."

Kylia laughed. "If only it were that simple."

"Isn't it?" Grant lowered his hand and set aside his scone, suddenly serious. "Are you telling me that you can't see into my heart?"

She shook her head.

He seemed almost relieved. "But you said you had seen me long before I came to your shores."

"Aye. For I have glimpses of the past and the future. But only glimpses, my lord. And not always when it is convenient."

That had him smiling. "I suppose it would be disconcerting to have a man's face suddenly appearing in your line of vision."

"Aye. Especially when I might be swimming, or riding amid the clouds on Moonlight's back, or even sleeping."

"I came to you in your sleep?"

She looked away. "Many times."

He didn't know why that should please him, but it did. "Did I ever speak to you?"

She shook her head. "I never heard your

voice until you washed up on our shore, but I..."

A chilling cry sounded from the depth of the forest.

Grant's hand was at the dirk at his waist even as he got to his feet and spun around.

"What was that, my lord?"

"I know not." He helped her to stand and led her away from the fire. "Keep to the shadows until I return."

Kylia felt her heart thundering as he walked away. Every minute that he was gone from her felt like an eternity. She imagined every sort of vicious creature lurking in the darkness, waiting to devour him. But as the silence stretched out, she began to fear that perhaps the barbarians had returned and had already attacked, leaving him alone and lying in his own blood somewhere in the forest.

He'd ordered her to stay. But what if he needed her? What good would she do him here, cowering in fear?

Just as she was about to follow, he stepped from the forest carrying a small bundle in his arms.

"What is this?" Kylia peered down at a mass of blood and matted fur.

"It appears to be a wolf pup. It must have wandered from the safety of its den and was attacked by a predator." Grant laid the pup down on the fur throw and began to pour the contents of his flask of water over the wounds. He looked up. "Puncture wounds. Deep. From the talons of an eagle, perhaps. I doubt the pup can survive. 'Twould be best if I ended its misery quickly."

Kylia knelt beside him and began to probe the wounds. She could feel the shallow breaths of the animal, and the trembling as shock set in. The pup's eyes closed, as though ready to accept its fate.

She moved aside their food and began wrapping the pup in the fur throw. Then she lifted the bundle in her arms and sat with her back against the trunk of a tree, crooning softly.

Grant dropped to one knee beside her. "You needn't do this, my lady. It's but a small creature of the wild. Death comes often here in the forests of the Highlands. You need to save yourself for the daunting task ahead."

She shook her head, sending dark curls dancing. "No life is insignificant, my lord. Even one such as this. Rest now, while I do what I can."

Instead of lying beside the fire he got to his feet and began to walk just outside the circle of firelight. He told himself it was because he wanted to see to their safety. But there was no denying the real reason. He needed to keep his distance from the lovely Kylia. Whenever he got too close, he was torn by the temptation to take what he had no right to. Just kneeling beside her, watching her cradle a wounded animal in her arms, had him thinking about things that were better left alone.

And so, while she rocked and crooned to a simple wolf pup, he stayed in the shadows and watched from a distance. And hoped with all his heart that when this was finished, and they had accomplished what they sought in his kingdom, he could return her to hers as he'd found her. Unspoiled by the evils of his world.

The night had grown silent. Except for the hooting of a nearby owl, and the gentle whisper of the breeze among the leaves, the forest creatures slept.

Kylia brushed a finger over the soft fur of the wolf pup and was rewarded by a quick lick of its tongue. This time when it closed its eyes, it wasn't to face death, but peaceful rest.

Drawing the fur throw around the sleeping creature, she laid it close to the fire for warmth before crossing the distance to the bubbling stream. There she knelt and scooped water to her mouth. Satisfied, she got to her feet and brushed down her skirts. As she turned, she saw a shadow looming over her and gave a gasp of alarm.

"My lord." Recognizing Grant, she sighed. "You startled me."

"Forgive me. How does the pup fare?"

"His wounds are healing. He's sleeping as peacefully as a baby."

"You should be doing the same. Our journey on the morrow will be long and arduous, if we're to reach my fortress before dark."

She tossed her head. "I'm not tired. In fact, I feel strangely invigorated. Perhaps it's the presence of the wolf pup." Even as she said the words, she felt shamed, knowing the pup was only a tiny part of these strange feelings. The real reason for the tumult in her heart was the man standing before her. He could rouse her, lift her, seduce her with but a look. Because it wasn't possible for her to lie, or even evade the truth, she blurted, "Nay, it isn't the presence of the pup. It's you, my lord."

He stepped back, eyeing her with a puzzled frown. "What are you saying?"

"I'm not feeling invigorated because of the wolf pup, but because of you." She took a step closer, narrowing the distance between them. She lifted a finger to his mouth. Just the merest touch, but she felt its repercussions clear to her toes. "It's knowing we're alone here."

Grant was determined to ignore the rush of heat. But there was no ignoring the way his heart was pumping furiously. "You're in a strange new land, far away from home and family for the first time, my lady. That is the only reason you can't sleep."

"Deny it if you must, my lord. But I know what my heart is feeling."

She saw him go very still.

When at last he spoke, even his tone was hushed. "What is your heart feeling, my lady?"

"Strangely elated. As though on the verge of some new and wonderful discovery." She traced the outline of his mouth with her finger.

He closed his hand around her wrist, stopping the movement. His eyes were narrowed on her with such intensity she felt a quick twist of fear.

"Do you know what happens when you tempt a sleeping wolf, my lady?"

When she said nothing, he whispered, "You become its prey. The wolf, once awakened, devours you."

He released her hand and turned away. His snub was like a knife to her heart.

Over his shoulder, he said softly, "Go now and rest for the morrow's journey."

Kylia felt tears spring to her eyes and brushed them away with the back of her hand. She watched as Grant took up his sword and stepped back into the shadows. As she started toward the fire, she blinked away the rest of her tears. She would not permit herself to weep over this man. Nor any man.

If she'd thought he would simply take what she offered, she was sadly mistaken.

She had, she realized, a great deal to learn about his world.

Chapter Ten

Grant stalked off into the darkness, filled with feelings of self-revulsion. He'd seen the pain in her eyes when he'd rejected what she was offering. But how could he allow himself to take advantage of her, when she had no idea what she was doing? If she wouldn't protect herself, someone had to. Foolish female. She'd spent a lifetime in paradise, where there existed no false pretense or dishonesty. How could she hope to survive in a land where such things thrived? Added to that, after only days away from her family, she had convinced herself that she was in love.

Love. If only it were so. He'd never met a finer woman. So sweet, so gentle, so generous with her gifts. It hurt him to hurt her, for she deserved only good things. But it was better this way. He would cut her off, quickly, deeply, to save her from even greater pain later.

But if her pain were anything like his, he hoped one day she would forgive him. For right now, this minute, he would give anything to forget about honor and integrity and simply take what she'd offered. He wanted her so desperately, it was a wonder that his heart was still beating. In truth, death would be preferable to this pain.

With a muttered oath he clenched the dirk at his side and almost prayed he would find some creature to fight. There was nothing like a good, satisfying battle to take his mind off what he really wanted to do.

Kylia drew her cloak around her and stormed back toward the campfire, her mind in turmoil. Was that how the lord of the MacCallum clan saw her? A foolish female seeking the thrill of a mere kiss?

She'd come offering him her heart. Did he have any idea what it had cost her to admit the truth? To bare her soul to him. Yet he had calmly, coldly rejected it. Rejected her.

He may have wrapped his rejection in pretty words about a wolf and its prey, but the meaning was perfectly clear. He didn't want her. Didn't want to be awakened from sleep to devour her.

Devour.

Kylia stopped in midstride as the meaning of his words washed over her. An aroused wolf devouring its prey.

Could it be that he hadn't rejected her love out of disinterest, but out of fear for her? She clapped a hand to her mouth as the realization dawned. He'd been protecting her. Her virtue. Afraid to take what she offered. Afraid that, by satisfying his own hunger, he would bring harm to her.

Her heart swelled with love for the man who would put her needs ahead of his own desire. No wonder his people had chosen him laird of their clan. Could they have found a more noble, honorable man than Grant MacCallum?

In her mind he had become a hero. A warrior and protector, determined to save her at any cost.

She turned back in time to see him disappear into the shadowy fringe of the forest, where he blended into the darkness. Moving quickly she followed.

Hearing the crunch of leaves and the snap of branches, he whirled, sword drawn.

When he saw that it was Kylia, his eyes narrowed. "You shouldn't be here."

She ignored the thread of anger in his tone. "I know now what you were doing."

He watched the uneven rise and fall of her chest as she struggled to calm her breathing. Nerves? he wondered. Or merely the exertion of following him?

"And what is it you think I was doing?"

"Protecting me, my lord."

His frown deepened. "Such a clever woman, my lady. If I'm not careful you'll soon uncover all my secrets, and figure out all the ways of my world, as well."

"Perhaps not all of them. But this much I know. You are not as disinterested in me as you pretend to be."

He couldn't hide his surprise. "And how would you know that?"

''For one thing, you have never once called me by name. Is it because you find my name so distasteful on your tongue? Or do you think, by refusing to do so, you keep a distance between us?''

For a moment he simply stared at her as he mulled her words. ''I think perhaps you're far too clever by half, my la—'' He stopped. ''I see what you mean. Very well. I'll agree to call you by name if you'll do the same for me.''

She swallowed and folded her hands primly at her waist before lifting her chin. ''Grant.'' It was spoken in a whisper.

The smile returned to his lips. This time he allowed it to reach his eyes. ''I can't hear you.''

She cleared her throat. Met his look. ''Grant.'' She spoke the word clearly. ''There you have it. And now mine, my lord.''

His smile faded, replaced by a frown. His fingers gripped the hilt of his sword until they were white. Why was this such an effort? He couldn't say. But he did manage to say, ''Kylia.''

''I don't believe I heard you, my lord.''

She was teasing him. He could see the laughter in those heather eyes. Teasing him as a maiden would tease a lover. The realization had him thrusting his sword deep into the ground before reaching out to close his hands around her upper arms and draw her closer.

"Kylia." His voice was a growl of pleasure and pain. "Kylia. Kylia. It is the loveliest name in the land. And I have long wanted to say it aloud."

He dragged her into his arms and pressed his mouth to the hair at her temple, breathing her in. "Kylia. My beautiful Kylia. As lovely as your name."

"Grant…"

He cut off her words with a kiss that seemed to steal her very breath. His mouth moved over hers, drinking her in, tasting, devouring.

She was caught by surprise. Always before, his kisses had been hesitant, almost reluctant. As though testing her, and allowing her to test him. To explore the unknown. But this time it was different. There was a boldness, a possessiveness about this kiss that had her head spinning, her heart thundering. He took it deep, draining her even as he filled her. As his arms tightened around her, he took the kiss deeper still, until she had no choice but to wrap her arms around his neck and give herself up fully to him.

"Grant."

"I love the sound of my name on your lips." He spoke the words against her mouth, then inside her mouth.

She couldn't catch her breath. Couldn't think. All she could do was hold on as his kisses took her higher and higher.

The hands holding her were almost bruising as they moved over her with a hunger that spoke to an answering hunger in her. And all the while that warm, clever mouth plundered hers.

She was hot where he touched her. So very hot. Yet icy needles slithered along her spine with each brush of his mouth on hers. She absorbed the rush of heat.

She moaned when he lifted his head, breaking contact. But instead of pulling away he merely changed the angle of the kiss and took it deeper, causing her to sigh with pleasure.

Her blood heated and pulsed and her breathing became ragged as his strong, clever hands moved over her, touching her everywhere, unlocking feelings she'd never even known existed. She wondered that her frantically beating heart didn't simply give up from exertion.

Grant could feel the change in her. She'd gone from surprise to a gradual awareness of herself as a woman. From surrender to desire. From desire to need. A need that was as compelling as his. Now what he wanted, what they both wanted, was within their grasp. They need only to take it.

Still he held back, concerned with her welfare. "Think, Kylia, what it is we're about to do."

"I can think of nothing else, Grant."

Nor could he. He nearly smiled, but this was far too grave an issue for levity. "Once we do this thing, we can never go back." He stared deeply into her eyes and saw the little fear that flickered there.

"You worry over me. Over my virtue."

"One of us must look out for you."

"Aye. And for that I'm grateful."

His tone roughened. "It isn't your gratitude I desire."

"Nay. It is this." She lifted her face to him. In her eyes was a look of such love, it nearly melted his heart. "I have no wish to go back, Grant. Only forward. With you." She lifted herself on tiptoe and pressed her mouth to his throat.

Such a simple gesture, but the tenderness of it was his undoing.

The blood roared in his temples. His vision was nearly blinded by a mist of passion. His heart beat a thunderous tattoo in his chest. With each touch of her, each taste, the need grew until he was beyond thought, beyond reason.

With a growl that seemed more animal than human he drove her back against the trunk of a tree and savaged her mouth with kisses that left them both gasping for breath. Though this change in him had her fearful, she clung to him, offering more, wanting him to end this terrible need inside her.

Needs unlike any she'd ever experienced writhed and twisted, demanding to be satisfied. Deep inside, a small fist pulsed and throbbed like a hollow ache. Her breasts felt swollen and tender, as her body strained toward his.

He ran hot, wet kisses along the smooth column of her throat, sending delicious curls of pleasure down her spine. But when his mouth dipped lower, to capture her breast, she could do nothing but gasp his name.

Despite the barrier of her gown, he nibbled and suckled until she moaned and writhed in his arms. "Grant, please…"

He lifted his head. "Do you wish me to stop?"

"Nay. I…" She couldn't speak over the dryness in her throat.

"Tell me that you want this, Kylia." He waited, afraid to breathe. If she should change her mind now, he would surely die.

There was a light in her eyes he'd never seen before. A gleam of desire that had her tossing aside her cloak and reaching up to twine her arms around his neck. She drew his head close for a slow kiss as she whispered against his lips, "I want this, Grant. Only this. And you. Only…"

He cut off her words with a kiss so hot, so hungry, it seemed to steal her breath.

And then there were no words as he tore her

gown aside in his haste. It pooled in the grass at her feet while he untied the ribbons of her chemise. As the fabric parted, he studied her in the moonlight. ''Oh, my sweet Kylia. You're even more beautiful than I'd imagined.''

He ran soft, nibbling kisses across her shoulder to her collarbone, then lower to her breast. He could feel the way she shivered, and he gathered her close, taking her nipple into his mouth.

She was seized with the most unbelievable wave of heat that nearly staggered her. She had a need to touch him as he was touching her. She reached blindly for him, and when her fingers fumbled, he helped her until his clothing joined hers in the grass at their feet.

He caught her hands and drew her down to her knees, before gathering her close to press kisses to her upturned face. He struggled to bank his needs as he kissed her eyelids, her cheeks, the tip of her nose. He could feel her relax in his arms as he ran his fingers lightly down her back, drawing her even closer, until his body was imprinting itself on hers.

''Do you know how much I want you, Kylia?''

When she didn't respond he drew her down, until she was lying beside him, with nothing but the cloak beneath to cushion her from the grass. "I would move heaven and earth for you, my lady. I would face the wrath of an army, or walk through a wall of fire, just to be with you."

She reached a fingertip to his mouth, tracing the outline of his lips. "I ask none of those things, Grant. I ask only that you feel about me on the morrow the way you feel about me this moment."

"I fear I cannot promise that, my lady." His eyes took on a light that had her heart stopping. "For I know that on the morrow my feelings for you will be even stronger."

"Oh, Grant." Her heart soared at his words.

He moved over her, touching her, kissing her, with a skill that had her shuddering with need. And though at first she was timid, she had a powerful need to touch him, as well. And did, until she heard his moan of pleasure. That only made her bolder, until she pressed her mouth to his throat and was rewarded by a wolfish growl from low in his throat.

He leaned over her, his eyes hot. "I warned

you, Kylia. Beware. For now that the wolf has been wakened, it will devour you.''

''I'm not afraid, Grant. For the wolf has been awakened in me, as well.''

They came together in a kiss that spoke of wild, primitive hunger. Of hard, driving need. Of desperate, raging passion. The forest that surrounded them no longer mattered. The night creatures that scurried through the brush were ignored. The wind that whispered in the leaves overhead went unnoticed. The darkness covered them with its mantle, shutting out the world. All they could hear was each labored breath. All they could feel was the heat that rose between them, clogging their lungs, leaving their bodies slick with sheen. All they could feel was this intense pleasure building, building with each touch, each kiss.

No man had ever touched her like this. One moment, so gently she nearly wept. The next, taking her on a wild climb until her heart was racing, her breath panting from between parted lips. Taking her higher, faster, until her head was spinning and her mind was so clouded she could no longer form a single coherent thought.

All she could do now was feel. The most incredible feelings as, with teeth and tongue and fingertips he drove her up and up until she thought she would go mad from the wanting. She didn't think it possible to want more. But each time she believed him ready to end this terrible need, he simply took her higher.

"Grant." His name was torn from her lips as she reached for him.

"Not yet, my love." He thought of all the things he'd dreamed of since meeting her. But none of them could compare with this. She lay in his arms, steeped in pleasure. Moonlight filtered through the branches of the trees, turning the ends of her hair to blue-black. Her eyes were glazed with passion. He could read the desire that mirrored his own.

The thought of taking her hard and fast had him trembling. He was desperate for release from this terrible storm building inside. But he wanted to give her so much more. He was determined to make this first time as pleasurable as possible. And so he brushed her mouth with his until the breath trembled from her lips.

He knew if he didn't soon end this torment,

he would go mad. And still he waited, lingering over her lips until she arched toward him. The press of her body to his was his undoing.

With a hoarse cry he entered then. He felt her stiffen and went very still.

"Forgive me, my love. I never meant to hurt…"

She cut off his words by dragging his head down for another kiss. And then she was wrapping herself around him, taking him in deeper, and he was lost.

He framed her face with his hands and stared into her eyes as he began to move. Half-mad with desire, she moved with him.

"Kylia. Oh, my lovely Kylia." He saw her eyes widen as she struggled to focus on him.

"Grant." His name was torn from her lips as together they began to climb higher, then higher still.

Their breathing was labored, their hearts pumping furiously as they soared to the heavens and shattered into millions of tiny stars.

Chapter Eleven

They lay, still joined, their breath coming hard and fast as they struggled to settle.

Grant pressed his mouth to her temple and tasted the salt of her tears.

Tears?

He rolled to one side and gathered her into his arms, brushing away the moisture with his thumbs. "I've hurt you. Forgive me, Kylia. It was selfish of me to want…"

"Nay." She touched her hand to his mouth to still his words. "You didn't hurt me. It was just so—" she searched for a way to make him understand "—incredible. Is it always like this?"

His poor heart took one hard bounce, then

returned to its natural rhythm. He'd feared it might never beat again.

"It is if the two lovers truly care about each other."

Lovers. The word caused a flutter in the pit of her stomach.

"And are we…?" She licked her lips. "Do you…?"

Seeing her confusion, he pressed his mouth to her temple. "We are and I do."

"You…love me?"

"Aye." He whispered the word against her mouth. "If you'll let me, I'll show you how very much I love you, my beautiful Kylia, in a hundred different ways. Starting with this." He ran kisses over her face, her throat, then lower, to her breast, and heard her rapid intake of breath.

Aware that he was fully aroused once more, she pushed away and stared up at him in surprise. "Is this possible? Again?"

He nibbled her neck, sending delicious tremors all through her body. "Not only possible, but extremely pleasurable, my lady."

"Aye." She shivered and wrapped her arms

around his neck, giving herself up completely to his ministrations. "You have the most amazing powers, my lord."

"You see, my lady. You're not the only one." The warmth of his laughter trickled over her senses as he drew her close and began to show her, in the only way he could, just what she meant to him.

As the night wore on, the two lovers were so wrapped up in each other, neither of them felt the way the wind picked up, chilling their heated flesh while sending the branches of the trees thrashing about wildly. Overhead, dark clouds billowed and boiled as thunder rumbled in the distance.

From deep in the forest came the chilling howl of a wolf. Grant lifted his head and struggled to hear over the wild beating of his heart. Just then lightning flashed across the midnight sky, followed by a rumble of thunder that shook the earth beneath them.

He dragged air into his lungs and waited for his head to clear. When he looked down at Kylia, he could see her struggling to calm her ragged breathing as well.

His first inclination was to curse the elements. Instead he touched a hand to her cheek. "It would seem that nature is against us, my lovely Kylia. From the sound of that thunder, we're directly in the path of the storm. It wouldn't be wise to remain here."

"Where will we go?" Her words were little more than a whisper.

"Since neither of us is in the mood to sleep now, I think we'd be wise to take up our journey until we find shelter." He caught her chin and tipped her face to stare into her eyes. "Do you believe me when I say I wish it were otherwise?"

Her breath came out in a long, slow sigh. "Aye. For I wish it, too. But I've no desire to be struck by lightning in a Highland forest."

"Especially when, by this time on the morrow, we'll be warm and dry within my fortress. My first concern must be your safety and comfort, my lady. My love," he added softly, sending her heart soaring.

When they were dressed he caught her hand and twined his fingers with hers, aware that both of them were trembling.

He took up his sword. "Come. We'll saddle the horse and be on our way."

When they reached the campfire, they saw the wolf pup still sleeping in his wrap.

Kylia looked down at the little mound of fur. "May I take him along?"

Grant looked doubtful. "He's a wild creature. He belongs in the forest with others like himself."

"But his wounds aren't yet healed. If we leave him here, he'll have no defense against his predators. Please, Grant. He's so small and helpless."

Grant looked into those pleading blue eyes and knew he'd already lost the battle. He would give her anything she asked, no matter the cost. "Bring him along. Though I've no doubt the hounds at my fortress will soon send him running back to the forest to escape their wrath."

"Perhaps he'll prove you wrong." She bundled the pup into her arms and moved along beside Grant as he carried the saddle toward his mount.

"So, my sweet Kylia." While he saddled his horse, he glanced at her. "Will the wolf become tame? Or will he lure the hounds to the wilderness?''

''Why can they not coexist? Who's to say they can't learn from each other?''

They both knew they weren't speaking only of the creature in her arms. They came from such diverse worlds. And yet, somehow, they'd managed to find common ground in their love.

He looked down at the little ball of sleeping fur. ''I suppose you've already given him a name?''

''Aye. Wee Lad.''

''Wee Lad. And what will you do when he's not so wee?''

''Then I shall call him simply Lad.''

''I suppose you'll start thinking of him as your child.''

''Perhaps. Who's to say?''

As rain pelted them, he lifted her to the saddle and pulled himself up behind her. When he took up the reins, he felt again the way his body strained toward hers.

This thing between them was far from ended. Loving her had only made him hunger for more.

He ought to be grateful for the storm. It

would keep his mind off the storm raging inside him. Even now, when he should have been sated, it was there. The thunder of need, the lightning of desire, the likes of which had never been seen before.

For now, he would have to be content to shelter her body with his, even though it meant hours of torment while he breathed her in and wanted her with a desperation that bordered on sheer madness.

The rain fell for hours while their horse picked its way across moss-covered boulders and slippery ravines. They kept to the cover of the forest, which offered them scant shelter from the storm.

By the time dawn painted the sky with touches of light, Grant pointed to a cave. ''We'll stop here awhile and refresh ourselves.''

Kylia was grateful when he lifted her from the saddle. She placed the pup on the floor of the cave and unfolded their precious bundle of food. Soon they were warmed by a fire, and soothed by the first food they'd eaten in hours.

Grant watched as Kylia offered tiny pieces of

cold mutton to the pup. After only a few bites the little eyes closed once more. Though weak, the animal seemed to be breathing easier.

Grant knelt before her with a knowing smile on his lips. "I know I promised to take you to the shelter of my fortress. But first, my love, I must taste your lips again."

She drew back, laughing. "You know where this will lead, my lord."

"Aye. Where it led us all through the night." He drew her close with a growl of pleasure. "But it's only an hour more. And this hunger is so great."

"It is the same for me…"

And then there were no more words as they came together in a firestorm of passion.

"I'll hold Wee Lad until you're seated, my love." Grant reached for the sleeping cub and helped Kylia into the saddle before pulling himself up behind her and handing her the precious bundle. He urged their mount forward, wishing he could spare Kylia this discomfort, for they were again facing into the bleak, bitter rain.

Not once had she uttered a word of complaint. Yet he'd felt her shiver, despite the warmth of her cloak.

Against her temple he muttered, "If you could but tame this weather, our journey would be easier. I suppose what I'm asking is only possible in your kingdom."

She turned her head slightly and gave him a smile. "Why didn't you say you wished the rain to stop? I thought perhaps your people needed it for their crops."

"They do. But I'd just as soon it rained on the morrow, so our journey today would be less tedious."

Kylia fell silent, and Grant concentrated on the steep trail ahead of them. He was surprised when, just minutes later, the rain ceased and the sun slipped from behind angry clouds.

"Did you do this?" His tone was incredulous.

"I wished it." She gave him a shy smile. "But I also asked my mum and gram to do what they could. Their powers are far greater than mine."

Grant shook his head. "You constantly amaze me, Kylia. What other powers have you failed to mention?"

She gave him an impish smile. "The truth is, I have no idea, for in my kingdom our powers seemed limitless. I just assumed everyone had them. Now that I'm in your land, I realize that much of what we took for granted there is absent here."

"How do you explain it?"

She shrugged. "Mum told us that there was a time when all people had the gifts of healing, of knowledge, of sight. But some abused their gifts, using them for personal gain. Some used their gifts against others, causing a great war that brought death and destruction to the land. Afterward, those who had started the war found their gifts had diminished. They became jealous of those who still had the gifts, and persuaded those like themselves to turn against the gifted ones, calling them witches. Many like us were hunted and killed. Others were imprisoned until they renounced their powers."

"And that's why your family fled to the Mystical Kingdom?"

Kylia nodded. "When we were just children, my sister Allegra took pity on the mother of a lad who had drowned. Allegra brought the lad back from that other world, and though his mother rejoiced, there were many who were scandalized. After being warned that we might be imprisoned as witches, we fled in the night.''

Grant shook his head. "What fools are we, that we would drive away the kindest creatures I've ever known?"

Kylia felt her heart swell at his words. Perhaps, if enough of his kind agreed with him, her family could one day return to this land and live without fear of punishment. It would be so grand to share their knowledge of healing, to put an end to war and hunger and mistrust among people.

But a part of her remained unconvinced. The barbarians they had encountered along the way had no desire for peace. And even one of Grant's own people had betrayed him. Was it possible to live in peace as long as there were evil ones among them?

"Look, Kylia." As they crested a ridge Grant reined in his mount and pointed.

"Is this your home?"

"It is. The village is known as Duncrune. My home is Duncrune Castle."

There was a softness in his tone, a tenderness that spoke, more than any words, what was in his heart.

She studied the rolling meadows, abloom with heather. In the valley was a lovely little village, with thatched-roof huts. Each home had a little garden and sturdy outbuildings. In the distance were green fields dotted with flocks of sheep. And standing on the highest ridge was a turreted fortress glistening in the afternoon sun.

She closed her hands over his, gripping the reins. "It's beautiful, Grant."

At her words he felt the curl of pleasure and knew that he'd been waiting for her reaction. It mattered more to him than he cared to admit.

"It has been in our clan for generations. And has been my home since I was born. It would pain me to lose it to another."

She turned slightly so she could look into his eyes. "You'll not lose your ancestral home to another. Not without a fight."

He couldn't help smiling. "You constantly surprise me, my lady. I didn't know you were capable of such fierceness."

"Only where you are concerned, my lord."

He bent close to brush a kiss over her cheek, sending heat spiraling down her spine. "Such loyalty. May it always be thus, Kylia. And may I always be deserving of it."

As he urged his horse along the village lane, and the people realized the laird had returned, they began waving and calling. Women peered from upper windows or paused while hanging their clothes to wave and shout. Crofters and tradesmen and farmers stopped their chores to lift their hats in greeting. Children halted their games to stare in openmouthed surprise as the laird and the fine lady rode past.

As Kylia watched, she had no doubt of the real warmth and affection of these people for their laird. They appeared to be truly delighted that he had returned to them. Who among them would betray him?

As the horse drew near the castle it broke into a gallop, eager for the comfort of its stable. They clattered into the courtyard and almost at once the doors were thrown wide and a handsome young man came rushing outside. Though not as tall as Grant, he was much wider both in shoulders and in girth. A spark of merriment lurked in his gray eyes as he shouted, "Grant. You've been gone too long."

"Aye, Dougal." Grant slid from the back of his mount and embraced the sunny-haired young man.

"Was the journey difficult?"

"It was. But well worth it." Grant turned and lifted Kylia from the saddle, keeping her within the warmth of his arms. "For look what my journey yielded." He caught her hand and led her closer. "Kylia, of the clan Drummond, this is my brother Dougal."

"Dougal." Kylia smiled shyly. "Your brother speaks lovingly of you."

"And well he should. For I'm his staunchest admirer." The younger man chuckled at his little joke. "Welcome, my lady." He pointed to the bundle tucked into the crook of her arm. "And what is this? Have you brought your bairn?"

That had both Grant and Kylia laughing.

"Not a bairn, but a wee pup." She opened the wrap to reveal the sleeping creature.

Dougal stepped closer, then looked startled. "A wolf?"

"Aye. He was wounded, and I couldn't leave him at the mercy of predators."

"She's named him Wee Lad. And I warn you, Dougal, she's begun thinking of the pup as a pet."

They looked up as Hazlet, wearing her usual nun's garb of black gown and veil, stepped into the courtyard.

"Aunt Hazlet." Grant crossed the distance between them to press a hand to her shoulder. "As you can see, my journey was successful. Come and meet the young woman who agreed to leave her Mystical Kingdom to aid in my search for the traitor."

The smile on his aunt's face faded as she lowered her voice. "You've actually brought a witch here to our home, Grant?"

"She isn't what you'd expect, Aunt. Come. Help me make her welcome." He placed a hand under her elbow and led her across the courtyard. "Kylia, of the clan Drummond, my aunt Hazlet."

Kylia's smile was warm. "Your nephew has spoken lovingly of you. How lucky he and Dougal are to have you in their lives."

"Indeed." Hazlet caught sight of the pup in her arms. "Is that what I think it is?"

"A wolf pup, Aunt. His name is Wee Lad." Dougal couldn't hide his delight as the hounds circled Kylia's feet, sniffing at the hem of her gown. One of the bolder ones actually stood on hind legs to sniff at the bundle in her arms, until Grant ordered it down. "I must warn you, my lady, that your pet could well become a tasty morsel for the hounds."

"Then I shall have to keep special watch to see that doesn't happen, Dougal, until he's big enough to do the same to them." Kylia watched as the servants gathered around Grant, bidding him a warm welcome home.

After greeting them with affection, he began the introductions. "I present the lady Kylia of the clan Drummond. My lady, this is Mistress Gunn, who has been housekeeper of Duncrune Castle since my father was a lad."

Kylia nodded toward the stick-thin little woman who dropped a curtsy as though meeting the queen.

When she straightened, Grant added, "Have the servants prepare the western wing for our guest, Mistress Gunn."

"The western wing? But that would put your guest in the chambers beside yours."

"Aye." He saw his aunt's stern gaze sharpen.

"This is our cook, Mester." Grant turned to a woman as round as she was tall, with a stark white linen apron tied around her ample middle. "Mester, the lady Kylia."

The cook bowed her head before wiping her hands on her apron and taking a step backward, as though afraid to get too close to a witch.

"Our stable master, Gresham."

Tall, gaunt, wearing his plaid tossed over a saffron shirt with voluminous sleeves, the man looked more like a preacher than a Highland stable master.

He doffed his cap and greeted Kylia with a long, assessing look, before saying, "Welcome, my lady."

He took up the reins of their horse and led it across the courtyard.

"And the man who has fought beside my father, and my father's father. Finlay MacCallum is a cousin to me, and a trusted friend."

Kylia's smile was as warm as sunshine. "Finlay."

"My lady." The old man's smile was equally warm. "I bid you welcome to Duncrune Castle."

"Thank you."

"Come inside and warm yourselves." The housekeeper pinched one of the serving wenches, who held the door and stood aside allowing them all to enter. "While Mester prepares a feast, I'll fetch tea and ale to the great hall."

As Kylia stepped inside, she drank in the sight of soaring staircases, highly polished banisters, and a massive chandelier with its hundreds of candles casting their light from ceilings high overhead, supported by massive wooden beams. Ancient tapestries, depicting the history of the MacCallum clan, lined the walls.

At the far end of the hallway were ornately carved doors leading to a chapel. The sweet smell of incense drifted from within.

Grant suddenly paused and caught Kylia's hand in his. Those around them looked on in startled silence as he lifted it to his lips and said almost reverently, "May you find the warmth of welcome in my home, my lady."

Chapter Twelve

At the sudden silence that fell over those around them, Dougal clapped a hand on his brother's shoulder. "You mustn't keep this lovely lady all to yourself." He turned to Kylia and offered his arm. "Permit me to lead you to our great hall, my lady."

Charmed by his boyish enthusiasm, Kylia laid a hand on his arm and walked beside him. Laughing, Grant offered his arm to his aunt.

She stepped back. "I'll be along in a moment."

Grant watched as she made her way to the chapel, where she dropped to her knees. With a shake of his head he trailed behind the others.

Once inside the great hall they settled themselves in chairs drawn close to the fire. Within minutes servants moved among them, offering ale to revive them after their arduous journey.

Kylia studied the crossed swords above the mantel, and the shield bearing the motto, *In ardua petit.*

She smiled. "He has attempted difficult things." She glanced at Grant. "Do these words speak of your father? Or one who went before him?"

"They refer to my father's father, who decreed that all those who follow would achieve greatness, if only they would attempt the difficult challenges."

"A noble heritage, my lord."

"Aye. Alas, my father died far too young to achieve the greatness he desired."

Hazlet, who had entered alone, arched a brow as she studied Kylia. "How is it that you can read the ancient words. Are you an educated woman?"

"My mother and grandmother saw to my education and that of my sisters. The ancient words are as familiar to me as the words we are now speaking."

Hazlet accepted tea from a servant. "Then you would understand the other motto of our clan, the one my nephew should have inscribed along with the words of our ancestor." She enunciated each word precisely. *"Deus refugium nostrum."*

Kylia nodded. "God is our refuge."

"I'm surprised you can speak His name, since everyone knows that witches worship devils."

"Aunt." As much surprised as annoyed, Grant set aside his ale. "I'll remind you that the lady Kylia is a guest of this fortress, and is here at my invitation."

Kylia touched a hand to his before turning to the older woman. "You need have no fear, my lady. I share the same beliefs as you."

"But surely you go against all that is good and holy by practicing your witchcraft."

Kylia saw the servants pause in their work to study her, and chose her words carefully. "What we do is share our gifts with those who have need of them. When your nephew came to our kingdom in search of aid, I offered to do what I could."

"Through witchcraft," Hazlet muttered as she folded her hands in her lap.

Attempting to smooth the rough waters, Dougal turned to his brother. "I want to hear all about your journey. Is there truly a dragon guarding the lady's kingdom?"

"Aye. Unfortunately, I was forced to slay it."

"A battle with a dragon." Dougal's eyes danced with undisguised excitement. "How I wish I could have been there to see it."

Grant felt the sting of remorse. "It's a pity that you were needed here in my stead, and weren't able to share the adventure. It is something I deeply regret."

"No more than I. But you were unharmed," Dougal said with a trace of pride. "And you've returned to those who love you."

Grant chuckled. "In fact, I was badly wounded. When first I confronted Kylia, I was so weak I fell at her feet. She and her family healed my wounds and made me welcome in their home."

"You are healers?" Hazlet's head came up sharply.

Kylia nodded. "We do what we can."

Dougal asked Kylia. "How did my brother persuade you to leave your kingdom and accompany him to the Highlands?"

She turned to Grant and the look in her eyes instantly softened. "I could see the goodness in his heart. That alone persuaded me."

Hazlet set aside her cup with a clatter. "You have yet to ask about your kinsmen, nephew. Have you no care about the safety of your people?"

Grant looked up. "Has there been an incident?"

"No one was harmed," Dougal said quickly.

"But our kinsmen were left without leadership while you pursued your folly. There have been sheep stolen in the night. An innocent lad was feared kidnapped by barbarians. The men of the Council have been muttering among themselves that their laird has failed them." Hazlet's tone lowered. "Dougal took charge as quickly as he could, but the people have a right to expect their laird to be here to put an end to these problems. There are those who believe it is time for you to step aside in favor of your brother."

"Aunt." Dougal's face reddened and he crossed the room to place a hand on his brother's sleeve. "I want you to know that I have no interest in taking your place as laird of our people. These few days have been enough to try my patience."

Grant smiled and patted his hand. "I thank you, Dougal." He lifted his head. "And you, Aunt. I thank you for your honesty. I will think on the words you've spoken, for the welfare of my people must be uppermost in my mind. If I believe in my heart that I am failing my kinsmen, I will surely step aside in favor of one who would better serve them."

He glanced over at Kylia, who was watching and listening in silence. "The lady will want to refresh herself." Grant offered his hand and Kylia got to her feet. "Perhaps, Aunt Hazlet, you'd care to show our guest to her chambers?"

His aunt shook her head, sending the ever-present veil drifting about her shoulders. "I must see that riders are sent out to the village to invite our kinsmen to your feast. They will want to see for themselves that you are indeed safely returned. Ardis will show the lady to her rooms."

A little serving wench stepped forward. "If you'll follow me, my lady."

Grant squeezed Kylia's hand. "Go along then. Ardis will return you to the great hall when the feast is ready. In the meantime, you'll have time to rest from your journey."

Kylia nodded. "Thank you." When she turned to thank his aunt, she saw only the hem of her gown as Hazlet hurried from the room.

She followed behind the little servant. At the top of the stairs they walked along a hallway lined with fresh tapers. The floors, Kylia noted, were spotless, as were the walls.

The young servant paused to open double doors, then stood aside while Kylia entered. Inside, the room smelled of beeswax and fresh rushes. A cozy fire burned on the hearth. In the sleeping chamber beyond, another fire burned, warming a lovely pallet lined with fur throws and fresh linens. A serving table nearby held a tray upon which rested a pitcher and basin.

Kylia turned to the servant. "This is lovely."

"Thank you, my lady." Ardis stood aside as a procession of servants entered. One folded a thick blanket in front of the fireplace, before positioning a tub on it. The others poured steaming water from buckets, until the tub was nearly full.

When they were gone, Ardis held out her arms. "May I take your burden, my lady?"

Kylia handed over the bundle and the wench gave a delighted laugh at the sight of the wolf pup yawning.

"You may place Wee Lad on my pallet, Ardis. He's still young enough that he requires a great deal of sleep."

"Aye, my lady." The wench set the bundle down, then helped Kylia remove her cloak, her boots and, at last, her gown and chemise.

Kylia stepped into the warm water and gave a sigh of pleasure as the little servant scrubbed her hair. "Oh, Ardis, I could stay here all night."

"Was it a difficult journey, my lady?"

Kylia realized that now that she had arrived at Grant's home, the trials and tribulations of their journey had slipped away.

"It matters not, Ardis. For now that I am here, I can put the journey behind me."

She stepped from the tub and wrapped herself in a thick blanket before settling on a chaise.

When she was comfortably seated, the servant poured strong hot tea and offered it to her.

"Rest now, my lady. I will come for you when it is time to dress for the feast."

"Thank you, Ardis." Kylia sipped the tea and stared into the flickering flames of the fire, before setting the cup aside and letting her head fall back.

Deliciously warm and content, she was soon fast asleep, with the wolf pup curled up beside her.

The dream was so real she could hear every clang of metal as sword met shield. Could feel every blow as the Highlanders and barbarians came together with clubs and dirks and finally, with their weapons lost on the field of battle, nothing but their fists.

She heard the voice of one, raised above the din. His face was so like the face of her love, his voice so familiar, she sucked in a breath in her sleep. "We fight to the death, lads. For the lives of all those we love are in our hands this day."

This, Kylia knew, was Stirling MacCallum, father of the man she loved.

She saw him take a knife thrust to the shoulder and reel in pain. In sleep she absorbed his pain and clutched her shoulder, as he clutched his.

"Ranald. Behind you." Despite his wound, he bent to retrieve a sword from the grass and attacked the one who had struck down his friend. As soon as he'd managed to run the barbarian through, he dropped his sword and knelt beside the man he loved like a brother. He brushed fair hair away from a face contorted in agony, and stared down into pale gray eyes. "Nay, Ranald. Hold on, my friend. I'll finish off these strangers and take you home."

Ranald's voice was soft, breathy, and oddly boyish for one so big. "I'm dying, Stirling."

"Nay. You cannot leave me. Think of Hazlet, my friend. Let her love give you the strength to live."

"If only I could. Be kind to her, Stirling, for she'll need your kindness, your strength, to see her through what is to come. Don't let her hide away in shame."

"Why should she be shamed? You fought like a true Highlander, Ranald. No greater love can there be than this, that you would give your life for those you love.''

The dying man shook his head. ''You know your sister's fierce pride.''

Stirling smiled. ''Aye. There are none prouder than Hazlet.''

''She'll retreat in anger and pain. Tell her...'' Ranald's voice was coming in short bursts now, as his life slowly drained away. His fingers curled around his friend's wrist as he struggled to say what was in his heart. ''Tell her to confide in your Mary, who has a kind and compassionate heart. And tell Hazlet I love her more than life itself.''

''You'll tell her yourself, as soon as...'' Stirling watched as the light went out of his friend's eyes and they stared vacantly. His own filled with tears and he caught Ranald to his chest, rocking him gently while he absorbed the pain of grief. ''...as soon as I take you home, my friend.''

It was a blow to his head that brought him out of his numbness and grief. Releasing his hold on his friend, he took up his sword and drove back the attacker, only to find two more. As he fought them off, three more appeared, and then a score, until his vision was filled with an army of barbarians, screaming and shouting as they moved in for the kill.

Standing alone, the bodies of his fallen comrades littering the field, he sustained more than a dozen wounds, any one of which would have killed a lesser man. But he fought valiantly until at last, bloody and beaten, his sword dropped from his nerveless fingers and he sank to his knees.

The barbarians were on him, with swords and clubs, until the grass ran red with his blood.

The pain was overwhelming now. So much pain he wanted to cry out. Instead he held his silence, robbing his enemy of their final triumph.

His last thoughts were of the love he felt for his wife, Mary, and infant son, Grant, as he gave up his life.

Kylia sat up with a jolt, her body fevered, her mind troubled. As awareness slowly dawned, the pain she'd been feeling receded. But though it diminished, it didn't entirely disappear. Bits and pieces of it remained with her, reminding her again of the price warriors paid so that those they loved could remain free.

The barbarians had invaded their land in order to take captives. The Highland men would be sacrificed so that the women and children would be enslaved. Their plans had been foiled by warriors like Stirling and Ranald. And were still being foiled by their descendants.

Though she was repulsed by the thought of war, she knew that without courageous warriors like Grant, and those who had gone before him, the future would be bleak for these good people.

Kylia stared into the fire, seeing in her mind the man who had looked so like Grant. The father he had never known. She knew that this dream had been visited upon her for a reason. She'd been given a glimpse into the minds of two men who had loved each other, had fought valiantly side by side, and had died together on the field of battle.

Was there some other reason for the dream? All her life she'd been gifted with the ability to see special people or events in dreams. Always they had been visited upon her for very specific reasons.

Perhaps in this case she'd seen Stirling and Ranald, and had felt their pain, because their loved ones needed to know that they had not died in vain.

She felt privileged to be able to tell those they loved just how courageous they had been. At her first opportunity, she would reveal her dream to Grant and Dougal, and their aunt. Though Hazlet made no secret of her distrust of Kylia's gifts, she would appreciate learning that the man she'd loved and lost had died like a noble warrior while, with his last breath, proclaiming his love for her.

It would surely go a long way toward easing the pain of her loss. Perhaps such a revelation would even help her throw off the garb of grief and return her mind and heart to the land of the living.

At a knock on her door, Kylia called out and smiled at the servant Ardis crossing the room.

Kylia felt indeed grateful for this gift. Because of it, she was about to lighten the burden of a woman who had been buried in grief for too many years.

Perhaps this, as much as finding the traitor, was her reason for being here. If she could bring peace to the hearts of those who grieved, her journey here would not have been in vain.

Chapter Thirteen

"Come, my lady." Ardis led the way across the room, where a number of garments had been arranged. "It is time to prepare for the feast."

After helping Kylia into an embroidered chemise of softest lawn, and several petticoats, Ardis pointed to the row of gowns. "What is your pleasure, my lady?"

Kylia sighed. "So many lovely things. Who provided all this?"

"My lord MacCallum." The servant dimpled. "He asked the village seamstresses to bring their wares, in the hope that some would fit you. Some may be too long, or too wide, but I will find a way to hide the imperfections."

"You're clever with needle and thread, Ardis?"

"Aye, my lady."

"As is my own mother. I was the bane of her existence because I could never master the art of sewing." Kylia pointed to a simple white gown. "I believe this one will do nicely."

The servant helped her into the dress, pleased to see that it needed nothing more than a sash to make it fit the lady's tiny waist. When Kylia was dressed, Ardis brushed her waist-length hair until it gleamed like a raven's wing in the firelight.

After draping a shawl of white wool, across her shoulders, the servant beckoned. "Now, my lady, I will lead you to the great hall."

"Thank you." Kylia lifted the bundled pup into the crook of her arm before following.

Ardis avoided her eyes. "I hope you won't take offense, my lady."

"At what, Ardis?"

"I don't believe the lady Hazlet will approve of an animal at table."

"Ah." Kylia glanced down at her tiny bundle. "Perhaps no one will notice. For he eats very little."

The young wench swallowed whatever else

she was about to say and offered no further advice.

As they descended the stairs, Kylia surveyed the great hall. "Everything is so clean and fresh. Mistress Gunn is to be admired."

"Aye. The lady Hazlet will not permit anything less than perfection in herself and those who serve her. She believes that Duncrune Castle must be worthy of the MacCallum clan, and to that end she oversees everything that Mistress Gunn and the household staff undertake."

"Perfection." Kylia seemed to mull that a moment. "I suppose it is what we all strive for, but few achieve it."

"The lady Hazlet comes closer than anyone, my lady."

"Does the lady Hazlet always dress like a nun?"

"Aye. 'Tis said that when she heard the news of Ranald's death, she donned the headdress and veil, and has worn it ever since. She lives a cloistered existence, leaving the fortress only to walk the gardens, where she prays. She has not once visited the village of Duncrune since the day the bodies of her brother and Ranald were brought home for burial. Each day she visits their tombs in the catacombs which lie beneath the chapel. She has said that her life without Ranald must be spent in prayer for his eternal soul.''

Kylia found herself moved to pity the woman who bore such grief alone. Now she was more convinced than ever that she must share the contents of her dream with Hazlet, in order to ease her pain.

Outside the doors of the great hall, the young servant paused and focused once more on the wolf pup in her arms.

In a low voice she whispered, ''You'd be wise not to offend the lady Hazlet. For she wields great power.''

''Aye. I'll keep that in mind. Thank you, Ardis.'' Kylia paused, then with a sigh, handed over her bundle. ''You're right, of course. See that he's given a few small morsels of meat and a bit of water, and is confined to my chambers until I return.''

''Aye, my lady.'' Relieved, Ardis took the pup from her hands and scurried away, as though eager to escape.

Kylia stepped inside the hall and was surprised at the number of men and ladies milling about, while servants threaded their way among the throngs, offering goblets of wine and ale. It would seem that the entire village and the surrounding hamlets must be empty of citizens this night. Again, Kylia thought, it was proof of how much the people loved their lord and wished to celebrate his safe return.

The minute Grant spotted Kylia he excused himself from those around him and hurried to her side.

His smile deepened. What a pretty picture she made, in the simple white gown and shawl, with her hair falling in soft waves to her waist. Just the sight of her had his heart growing lighter.

"My lady." He caught her hand and lifted it to his lips. "Were you able to rest?"

"Aye. And you?"

He shook his head. "I'd hoped to come to you in your chambers." In truth, he'd wanted desperately to be alone with her for just a few moments. He sighed. "But there was no time. There was much to discuss with my brother and aunt, before meeting with the Council."

Kylia thought she detected a flicker of weariness in his eyes, but before she could offer a word of comfort she found herself immediately surrounded by curious onlookers.

Grant called for silence before saying, "May I present the lady Kylia, of the clan Drummond." The note of affection in his voice had many in the crowd straining to see this mysterious stranger.

A tall, dark-haired warrior stepped forward. "I am Culver, cousin to Hazlet. My mother and hers were first cousins."

"Culver." Kylia smiled as he took her hand in his.

He lifted it to his lips. "My cousin tells me you are from the Mystical Kingdom."

"Aye. That is my home."

He seemed surprised by her easy acknowledgment. "It's true then, that you are a witch?"

Many in the crowd gasped at his utterance. Though many had whispered about her behind their hands, none would have dared speak the word aloud.

Before she could respond, a red-bearded giant

pushed his way toward her and caught her hand in his, lifting it to his lips. "The clan Drummond, you say?" His booming voice carried clearly over the other voices in the room. "'Tis an ancient, noble clan indeed, with a proud heritage."

Kylia gave him a grateful smile. "I know not your name, sir."

"Lord Giles MacCallum. Though our land lies on the far banks of the loch, we have fought side by side with our cousins since the days of Stirling MacCallum, to keep our Highlands free of barbarians."

"You knew the lord's father?"

"Aye. And his friend, Ranald."

At the mention of that name, Hazlet crossed herself and turned away, causing many in the room to pity her.

"It's time we partook of the feast prepared by Mistress Gunn and our cook, Mester. Come, my lady." Grant offered his arm and Kylia placed a hand on his sleeve. He turned to the older man. "Giles, you'll join us at table?"

"Aye, my friend. I'd like nothing better than to get to know this lovely lady better." The old warrior offered his arm to Hazlet. "Will you do me the honor, my lady?"

"Nay." She shrank from his touch and turned away. "I must first see to the servants. But I'll be along shortly."

"A pity your aunt can't enjoy herself as other women do." Lord Giles MacCallum dropped an arm around Dougal's shoulders and the two followed Grant and Kylia through the crowd until they'd reached the head table.

Grant took the place of honor at one end of the long table, with his man-at-arms Finlay at the other end. Kylia on his left and his brother on his right. Lord Giles eagerly sat on the other side of Kylia and immediately engaged her in conversation. By the time Hazlet arrived, trailed by her cousin Culver, the servants had begun making their way to the tables with trays of pheasant, salmon and mutton, along with baskets of bread and goblets of ale.

Hazlet took her place beside Dougal and fell silent, bowing her head until the others at table followed suit. Though she spoke no words aloud, her lips moved and the others waited respectfully until she lifted her head and accepted food from a servant.

"Now." Giles leaned toward Kylia. "I must hear all about your Mystical Kingdom, for I've heard the stories since I was but a lad."

"What did you hear, my lord?" Kylia helped herself to a piece of fish.

"About dragons and monsters and all manner of fearsome guardians of your kingdom."

"That much is true, my friend." Grant sipped his ale. "For I first had to slay the dragon before crossing the Enchanted Loch."

"Is it enchanted?" Giles arched a brow.

"It would seem so. I saw water that not only sparkled like diamonds, but was filled with the precious stones. And then rubies, as the dragon's blood was spilled into it."

"A trick of the mind." Hazlet's eyes narrowed with indignation.

"I know what I saw, Aunt." Grant thought about the jewels he carried in a tiny pouch in his tunic. Though they would prove the truth of his words, he was reluctant to share them with others, for they were special to him.

He turned to Giles. "I was so weak I should have drowned, but the water refused to let me sink. Instead I was allowed to drift until I reached the far shore, where I fell at the lady's feet.''

The others around the table were silent, watching and listening. Most were fascinated by all they heard.

''What other amazing things did you see, my lord?'' Culver glanced at Kylia. ''We wish to hear everything.''

Grant deliberately refrained from any mention of the fairies and winged horses, knowing there were some who might be willing to risk the fierce guardians of the Mystical Kingdom in order to steal such treasures. This world was filled with unscrupulous men who would use such innocent creatures for their own gain. Likewise he made no mention of their experience in the Forest of Darkness. It was, like the dragons and monsters, a barrier that stood between his world and Kylia's. He did, however, recount their harrowing encounter with the barbarians, and Kylia's courage.

All who heard were amazed that this lovely, gentle woman could reveal such strength of purpose.

''Were you not afraid, my lady?'' Giles tugged on his beard.

"I was. But I was even more afraid of doing nothing, for that would surely have doomed us both."

"You should have seen her." Grant described the way Kylia controlled the barbarians with lifted arms, until the two of them were able to make their escape. "The lady was magnificent."

As his narrative continued, Hazlet's frown deepened, revealing just how repulsed she was by the images conjured by her nephew's tale.

"Dragons. Monsters. What nonsense. It is obvious you were under a spell, nephew, for we all know such things do not exist."

"Perhaps not in our world, Aunt, but I saw them with my own eyes." He turned to wink at Kylia. "I saw other things too amazing to speak of, for you'd then swear I was daft."

While the others laughed, Hazlet pursed her lips. "Perhaps you are still under a spell, nephew."

Giles made an attempt to lighten the older woman's mood. "And why not? When a young, healthy warrior meets a maiden as lovely as this, how can he help but fall under her spell? I believe I've fallen as well, my lady, though I'm well past my prime."

Hazlet got to her feet. "Such ribald remarks are beneath you, Giles, and insult me, since you know I tolerate no levity concerning the baser instincts."

"Please, Aunt. You know Giles meant no harm." Dougal attempted to lay a hand on her arm, but she pushed it aside.

"You would take up sides with these others?"

"Aunt, I was merely…"

She lifted a hand to silence him. "I know how easy it is for a man to be led astray by a coarse woman. But I'd hoped those who bear the name of MacCallum were better than most." Her gaze swept those at table, pausing to linger on Kylia before moving on to Grant, and then to Dougal. "It would seem I was wrong."

She turned away and walked from the great hall, looking for all the world like a queen among peasants.

As soon as she took her leave, the room was abuzz with speculation about the lord's unwelcome houseguest, and the lady who was the acknowledged mistress of Duncrune Castle.

Grant leaned close to Kylia. "I hope you can find it in your heart to forgive my aunt. She labors under a heavy heart."

Overhearing, Giles gave a grunt of displeasure. "Aye, and woe to anyone who tries to forget it. The lady not only suffers her grief, she embraces it. Welcomes it. Wears it, along with her nun's habit, to keep it fresh in her mind and ours."

"Giles…" Grant shook his head, but it was too late.

The old man's words had Dougal getting to his feet to defend the object of his scorn. "Though it may be true that our aunt grieves, who's to say when a broken heart will heal? Her pain is real, Giles, and I hope you will be gentleman enough to retract your accusation here and now."

The older man nodded. "Forgive me, Dougal." He turned to his host. "And you, my lord. It was not my intention to disparage your beloved aunt."

Satisfied, Dougal took his seat.

Culver pushed away from the table and bowed to Grant. "Your brother is right, my lord. Your aunt must be feeling abandoned by all who love her. By your leave, I'll go after her and keep her company, so that we don't add to her grief.''

''That's kind of you, cousin.'' Grant nodded his approval. ''You're excused, Culver.''

As he walked from the room they returned their attention to their meal. Soon, with the help of Giles's gentle teasing, they were once again laughing among themselves and sharing tales of battles and adventures.

As the conversation swirled around her, Kylia thought about what Giles had said. Could Hazlet not see that her expressions of grief were creating a chasm between her and those who loved her?

She realized with a trace of sadness that Hazlet's absence brought a sense of relief to everyone in this hall. Without her dour countenance they could enjoy the levity of this happy occasion without guilt.

Chapter Fourteen

As the night wore on and the ale flowed, the guests became more raucous. It was impossible to take more than a bite of salmon or taste of mutton before pausing for another speech and an emptying of goblets, only to have them filled once more by passing servants.

Though Hazlet never returned, her friend and cousin, Culver, moved through the crowd, head bent in earnest conversation with many of the men from the village.

"M'laird." A bleary-eyed warrior shuffled to his feet. "It's come to my attention that ye left yer people without protection for many days while ye were off fetching the lady seated at yer table."

Grant nodded. "Aye. My journey took many days. But the lady kindly offered to accompany me to my home to lend her services."

"And what would those services be?"

At his coarse suggestion, the crowd fell silent.

Anger flared in Grant's eyes, though he managed to bank it. "The lady has the gift of healing and sight."

"A witch," someone muttered aloud.

"How do we know ye aren't under her spell?" another shouted.

"Aye." A barrel-chested warrior got to his feet and tossed aside his goblet. "How do we even know yer the same man who left Duncrune Castle all those days ago? If ye're in the company of a witch, how do we trust that ye'll still protect us? I say we should choose another laird from among those present. One whose mind isn't clouded by witchcraft."

The bleary-eyed warrior took up the challenge. "If yer father were alive, Grant MacCallum, we'd have no such decision to make. Now there was a man who knew how to fight his enemies."

"Aye." A shout went up that nearly shook the rafters.

"We deserve a laird who can make us all proud as well." The warrior's voice trembled with emotion.

The men and their ladies drank, then pounded their cups on the wooden tables to attract the attention of the harried servants.

"We demand an answer, m'laird." The warrior's voice was roughened by ale and anger. "Did ye tarry along the way with the witch? Is that why ye left yer people so long without protection?"

"You desire an answer?" When Grant's hand went to the sword at his hip Kylia closed a hand over his.

Her voice was a low, quiet plea. "This isn't the way, my love."

"It's the only answer I'll give them. If they choose to turn against you, they turn against me, as…"

His words faded as a group of strangers strode into the great hall. At the sight of them, the crowd fell silent.

"I come seeking Laird Grant MacCallum." The booming voice of the leader carried to the rafters of the hall.

Grant stepped closer. ''I am the man you seek.''

The leader extended his hand. ''I am Burke, laird of the clan Kerr. I was off in battle with an army of barbarians, and have only now learned that you and the lovely lady Kylia saved the life of my son, Ewald, and his wife and family. Had it not been for your kindness, I now know that they would have perished at the hands of the thieves who raided their flock and burned their cottage. My people told me of your goodness, and that of your lady. How the two of you stayed, without sleep or shelter, protecting them and their flock until my son was strong enough to be returned to his village. Even then you didn't abandon him, but accompanied him home before taking up your journey once more.''

He turned and directed his men to step forward, bearing one cask of ale, and another of gold.

Grant couldn't hide his astonishment. ''You are too generous, Burke of the clan Kerr.''

''No more than you, my laird. For my son and his family are more precious to me than gold.'' He looked beyond Grant to where Kylia watched in silence. ''Is this your lady?''

"The lady Kylia of the clan Drummond."

"Drummond?" Burke's smile widened. "Your clan is ancient and noble, my lady. I have heard of your healing powers, and I am grateful." He lifted her hand to his lips. Then he turned to Grant. "In gratitude for your kindness, I pledge my loyalty, and that of my warriors. Should you find your land under siege, you need only send word and we will come with all haste."

He turned and, flanked by his warriors, began to withdraw.

"Wait." Grant extended his hands. "Stay and refresh yourselves."

The older man shook his head. "These are dangerous times in our Highlands. There are invaders everywhere. I dare not leave my clan without my protection."

With that he strode from the hall.

In the stunned silence that followed, Dougal stood and faced the crowd. "Let this be an answer to any questions that linger. There can be no doubt that Grant MacCallum is the finest, noblest laird in the Highlands, for he risked his own life for that of a stranger in need. But besides being a noble laird, there's also no finer brother in the Highlands than mine.'' He raised his goblet. ''To my brother. My laird.'' He drained his ale before adding, ''I pledge my heart and my sword.''

''As do I, lad.'' Giles stood and raised his sword to the ceiling.

''As do I.'' Finlay, looking grave, added his voice.

''Highlanders proud and free.'' The men, caught up in the spirit of the moment, leaped up shouting the words over and over. Soon their women were standing as well, adding their voices to the chorus.

Grant looked over at Kylia and saw the glimmer of tears on her lashes. He caught her hand and drew her up beside him before brushing a kiss to her palm. ''Why do you weep, my lady?''

''I worried over you, my lord. And yet what I hear now tells me that your people have great affection for their laird.''

He continued holding her hand in his as he acknowledged the cheers of his people. Then, as they finally took their seats, he leaned close to whisper, "I can't allow myself to forget that there is one among them who would betray me. And, despite the will of the people, there is the Council to consider."

"The morrow is soon enough to think about that, my lord." She smiled up at him, her tears forgotten. "Tonight you should enjoy the fruits of your labors. For you have returned to the bosom of your people, and they will sustain you through whatever trials are to come."

Grant threw back his head and laughed. A rich, warm sound that wrapped itself around her heart. "How have I lived so long without your sweet goodness, my lady? You almost make me believe that you can soften even the most hardened of hearts."

She touched a hand to his. "Believe it, my lord."

As they returned their attention to the feast, the others at the table found themselves watching these two handsome young people, aware that their relationship was much more than that of two friends. For the love that gleamed in their eyes was impossible to hide.

The challenge boldly tossed by one warrior

was now on the minds of all. Had their laird lost his heart to a witch?

Grant stood by the doors of the great hall, bidding his guests good-night. Servants scurried about fetching cloaks and shawls, while Gresham and the stable lads woke grooms who'd fallen asleep after finishing their pints behind the stables.

Those warriors who could still sit a horse were helped into their saddles, while the rest climbed into the backs of wagons and carts for the ride back to the village with their ladies.

Throughout all the commotion, Grant was aware of Kylia standing in front of the fireplace, talking softly to Dougal, Finlay and Lord Giles. The sight of her, so calm and serene amid the chaos, did strange things to his heart.

"I bid you good-night, cousin." Culver accepted a cloak from a servant and started away.

Grant laid a hand on his sleeve. "How is my aunt?"

"She is calmer of mind now. A servant brought us a meal, and afterward she visited Ranald's tomb to pray. I believe she regrets her display of emotion, cousin."

Grant nodded. "Will I see you on the morrow?"

"Aye, for Hazlet has asked me to break the fast with her."

"You are welcome at my table, Culver."

"I thank you, cousin." The man turned away and strode out the door to the courtyard.

Minutes later Grant joined the others by the fire. "Will you stay the night, Giles?"

The older man shook his head. "I have business in the village. But I'll return on the morrow, for we have much to discuss with the Council before I leave for my home." He offered his hand to Grant, and then to Dougal and Finlay, before turning to Kylia. "My lady, I am honored to meet you."

"And I you, Lord Giles."

He lifted her hand to his lips before taking his leave.

Kylia climbed the stairs between Grant and Dougal, who accompanied her to the door of her chambers, where she was greeted by Ardis.

"Good night, my lady." Grant bowed formally over her hand before lifting it to his lips.

His brother did the same. "Good night, Kylia.

I can't wait to hear more about your kingdom on the morrow.''

When they were gone, Kylia walked to her sleeping chambers and slipped the shawl from her shoulders.

"You must be weary, Ardis.''

"Nay, my lady. Whenever there is a feast here at Duncrune Castle, I get the chance to visit with my kin from the village.''

"Are there many?'' Kylia stepped out of her gown and petticoats and accepted the nightdress of softest lawn.

"Aye. My mother was one of seven, my lady. And my father the eldest of five. After the guests are fed, we gather in the refectory to eat and talk endlessly until we catch up with all the news of our families.''

Kylia found herself smiling at the image. "That sounds like such a grand time. Whenever my sisters and I get together, we never seem to run out of things to talk about.''

"Aye. It is the same with us. Will I help you into your pallet before I leave?''

"Nay, Ardis. I'll see myself off to my bed in a few moments.''

"Then I'll say good-night, my lady " Ardis picked up one of the candles and made her way out.

When the door to the chambers closed behind the servant, Kylia walked barefoot to the balcony to watch the clouds drifting across the star-studded sky.

It soothed her to know that those same stars were winking over the Mystical Kingdom.

"Are you watching, Mum? Are you missing me as I'm missing you?"

The light of one star seemed to grow brighter than all the rest, and Kylia watched as it began to dance in the night sky. It lasted for only a few moments, before the star returned to its place in the heavens, and its light gradually dimmed. But when it was over, Kylia found herself smiling.

"Thank you, Mum. I don't feel quite as lonely now."

She turned and was startled by a tall, shadowy figure behind her. She covered her mouth with her hand to stifle the little cry that sprang to her throat, then slowly let out a sigh of relief. "Grant. You startled me."

"Forgive me, my lady. I wanted to be certain your servant was gone before showing myself."

"You shouldn't be here. Surely someone will see you, and by morning we will be the talk of the castle."

"Trust me, my lady, we are already the talk of, not only the castle, but the entire village of Duncrune. Do you mind?"

She shook her head and the dark silk of her curls drifted like a veil around her shoulders. "Not for my sake. But for your sake, you should leave, Grant. After all, you are laird of the castle."

"And as laird, I choose to be here with you." He reached out a hand to her hair and watched as the strands sifted through his fingers. "All night I wanted this. Only this." He took her hand and placed it over his heart. "Feel what you do to my poor heart."

"It's thundering."

"Aye." He looked into her eyes before drawing her close and brushing her mouth with his. "The need for you is such, my lady, that I couldn't bear the thought of sleeping alone."

He kissed her long and slow and deep, until

she sighed and wrapped her arms around his neck, giving herself up to the pleasure.

It was what she wanted, as well. Just this. To be held in this man's arms. To feel treasured above all else. To be loved until they were both sated.

"My people were charmed by you, Kylia." He ran soft kisses across her temple to her cheek. "My brother Dougal could hardly contain his excitement at meeting you." He pressed a kiss to the tip of her nose. "It was clear that Finlay and Giles were enchanted by you."

She moved until her mouth found his, hungry for more of his kisses. "And their laird?"

"Has lost his heart to you completely, my lady."

They came together in a kiss so hot, so hungry, the very air around them seemed charged with energy.

"So." The sound of Hazlet's voice had their heads coming up sharply. "This is how the laird of Duncrune Castle behaves when in the company of a witch."

Kylia started to step away when Grant's hand on her shoulder stopped her. Holding her close, he looked over. "You are intruding, Aunt."

"I can see that, for I have eyes. But it seems my nephew has been blinded by witchcraft."

"I prefer to call it love." His tone was soft, but there was no denying the barely controlled anger that lay beneath.

"Do not debase the word with such as I have just witnessed, nephew. Love is only true when blessed by the sacraments, and witnessed by a man of the church. What you and this witch share is coarse and base, and mocks everything that is good and decent."

Grant heard Kylia's little intake of breath and absorbed her pain to his own heart. With an oath he set her behind him before advancing toward his aunt. "You will leave these chambers, never to return. Do you understand me?"

"You need not bar me, for I have no desire to see this woman, or speak to her again. She is a vulgar woman who is leading you down a path of destruction, nephew. Fool that you are, you are so blinded by her beauty, you fail to see the evil that lurks in her heart."

As she turned away, Kylia hurried across the room to bar her exit from the room. "Wait, Lady Hazlet, for there is something I must tell you."

The older woman shoved her aside and flung open the door. On the threshold she turned. Though it was impossible to see her eyes through the ever-present veil, the venom in her voice was plain enough. "You are dead to me. As is my nephew. I will hear no evil words from your lips. Nor will I acknowledge you in any way."

She turned to Grant. "Beware, nephew. I wield great power with the Council. Greater than any witch." She turned away and called over her shoulder, "You will rue the day you brought this creature to Duncrune Castle."

As her footsteps echoed in the dark hallway, Grant closed the door and drew Kylia into his arms. Against her temple he whispered, "I misjudged the depth of my aunt's grief. Giles was right when he said it had taken over her mind." He tipped up Kylia's chin and stared into her troubled eyes. "Don't let her words turn you against me, my love."

"How could I ever?"

"Promise?"

"Aye. But I ask a promise of you in return."

"Anything."

She sighed. "Don't shut your aunt out of your life."

He drew back. "You heard the words she hurled at me. At us. She insulted the woman I love. How can I continue to allow her to do so?"

Kylia touched a finger to his lips. "Listen to me, my love. For all Hazlet's anger, I feel she is deeply troubled by something from her past. Perhaps she fears that Ranald didn't love her enough. If that's so, I can assure her he did."

"And how do you know that?"

"Come." She caught his hand and led him toward her pallet. "I'll tell you about my dream."

The smile was back in his eyes; the warmth in his voice. "Aye. I'll gladly listen." He drew his arms around her waist and pressed his lips to the hollow of her throat. "And when you've finished, I'll show you all the wonderful things I've been dreaming about."

Chapter Fifteen

"My lady."

A knock on the door of her chambers, and a muffled voice from the other side, had Kylia sitting up in confusion. Beside her, Grant folded an arm beneath his head and frowned.

His voice was sleep roughened. "Tell Ardis to go away."

Kylia looked alarmed. "How can I do that, my lord? It's her duty to help me prepare for the day."

He drew her down and brushed a kiss over her cheek, sending heat curling all the way to her toes. "Tell her to come back when the sun is high."

Kylia lifted her head and glanced at the balcony. "It's been raining all night. The sun may not come out for hours."

"Even better." He ran a hand down her hair and growled against her lips, "Send her away. I'm not ready to leave you, my love."

Kylia sighed. "I simply cannot lie."

"Then tell her the truth."

Seeing the challenge in his eyes, she turned to the door and called, "Come back later, Ardis. I'm not ready to leave my pallet yet."

"Aye, my lady."

As Ardis's footsteps receded, Kylia caught sight of the wide smile that split Grant's lips. "That was no lie, for I'm not ready to leave yet."

"A good thing." He dragged her into his arms and kissed her until they were both breathless. "For after that dream you shared with me last night, I'm feeling even more inclined to spend every precious day doing something pleasurable, in order to store up memories for the bad times."

"What makes you think there will be bad times, my lord?"

"Right now—" he ran soft, wet kisses down

her throat "—it's impossible to think at all, my love."

And then, as the castle hummed with activity beyond the door, the two of them slipped away to a warm, snug cocoon of soft sighs and gentle kisses.

"Good morrow, Grant." Dougal hurried across the great hall to clap a hand on his brother's shoulder before bowing to Kylia. "My lady. I hope you slept well on your first night under our roof."

"I did, thank you." Kylia could feel her cheeks color as she walked to the table between Grant and his younger brother. She looked up at the men who were awaiting them at table. "Good morrow, Finlay, Culver. Lord Giles."

The three men were on their feet and bowing over her hand.

"My lady." Giles beamed. "You are truly a sight for these old eyes."

"You say that to all the pretty maidens," Finlay said dryly. He turned to Kylia. "But in your case, my lady, the man does not exaggerate. You look refreshed."

"I am, thank you." She took her seat beside Grant and accepted a goblet of hot mulled wine from a servant.

Grant turned to Culver. "Where is my aunt?"

"She decided to break her fast in her chambers." The older man looked uncomfortable as he added, "She thought it best."

"Will you convey to her that I desire her company at table when we sup tonight?"

"I will, my lord." Culver seemed surprised and more than a little pleased. "Does this mean that you bear her no ill will?"

"I'm still smarting from her words, but the lady Kylia begged a favor, and I cannot refuse. For the sake of this good woman, I request my aunt's company."

Culver bowed slightly to Kylia. "You are as wise as you are lovely, my lady." He turned to Grant. "By your leave, I'll convey your request to your aunt now."

Grant nodded. When the man was gone, he glanced around the table at the others, who had listened in silence.

Dougal seemed relieved. "I'm glad you're willing to forgive our aunt, my lady. For she's been like a mother to us all these years."

"So your brother has told me. And like a mother, she is fearful of what she doesn't understand. My family has long known that we are feared in your world because of our gifts."

"Tell me about them." Dougal began polishing off a joint of fowl, while emptying his goblet. He ate with a boyish enthusiasm that had Kylia grinning.

Seeing her watching him, he paused. "What is it, my lady?"

She shook her head. "It's just that I'm unaccustomed to seeing anyone eat with such glee."

"Don't the men in your kingdom enjoy their food?"

Again she laughed. "There are no men in the Mystical Kingdom. Well, except for Jeremy, but I'm not sure a troll is the same as a man."

"A troll?" The food was forgotten as he stared at her in surprise. "There truly are such things as a trolls?"

"I know of only one."

"Aren't they nasty little mythical creatures that sleep under bridges and live off the kindness of others?"

"Jeremy is as sweet as a bairn. Though he has confessed to being quite angry when he lived in this world. But he has forgiven those who taunted him. As has Bessie."

"Is Bessie a troll, too?"

"Nay." Kylia laughed, a clear sweet sound that had Grant smiling along with her. "Bessie looks like an old crone, all stooped over, with a hunched back and crooked, almost fearsome features, but she cooks like an angel and has the disposition of a saint. Before my family fled this land, we encountered Jeremy and Bessie living in dire circumstances, and made them part of our family. When we left for our kingdom they chose to go with us, since they had nowhere else to go."

"You weren't afraid of them?" Dougal asked.

"Nay. For my mum and gram taught us that we must look beyond the face that one shows to the world, and see what is in the heart."

Giles shook his head. "You continually surprise me, my lady. If all of us could follow that advice, this world would be a better place."

Dougal polished off yet another joint of fowl

and leaned back. "I want to hear all about your kingdom, my lady."

"Another time." Grant drained his goblet and got to his feet. "Now we must meet with the Council, for there is much business to discuss." He touched a hand to Kylia's shoulder. "Perhaps you'd care to explore the castle a bit, my lady."

She closed a hand over his. "I'd like that."

As they started away Giles paused. "The castle gardens are lovely this time of year, my dear. I've heard you have a wolf pup that might enjoy the freedom to run."

"Aye. I've named him Wee Lad. I thank you, Lord Giles."

Kylia watched them walk away, then got to her feet. Hadn't Culver said that Hazlet walked the gardens each day while she prayed? If she were ever to make peace with the woman, she'd best start now.

The rain had fled, leaving the gardens green and the stones that lined the pathways sparkling in the sunlight. Wee Lad ran ahead, stopping to sniff at all the strange, new things. As Kylia followed more slowly along the hedgerows, she was soon caught up in the peace of her surroundings. Roses grew in profusion, as well as colorful foxglove, lady's mantle and fragrant lavender. There were fountains where birds splashed, and stone benches inviting her to pause and enjoy the beauty. While the pup chased a butterfly, she sat, listening to the flow of water and filling her lungs with the wonderful perfume of the flowers.

It pleased her to know that the people in Grant's world enjoyed the same simple pleasures that she had always enjoyed in hers. She smiled at the antics of Wee Lad as he stood very still, watching a family of birds that spread their wings and hopped about, enjoying their bath.

She was so lost in the sight of the pup's antics, as he dashed into the fountain and chased the birds, she was startled when a robed figure entered her line of vision. Hazlet, in the familiar veil and headdress, walked with her head down, her lips moving in silent prayer.

When she caught sight of Kylia seated on the stone bench, she looked around wildly, as though planning to flee. Then, seeing that she'd been spotted, she lifted her head and fixed Kylia with a stern look. "What game do you play with me, witch?"

"Game?" Kylia sat up straighter.

"Culver told me that my nephew requests my presence at his table, because you asked it of him. Why would you do such a thing?"

"You are as much mother as aunt to Grant and Dougal. It would pain them to be separated from you."

"Why should that matter to you?"

"You are a woman who loved a man deeply. You, more than anyone, ought to understand that anything that causes pain to Grant, pains me as well."

"You dare to pretend to care about my nephew the way I cared about my beloved Ranald?"

"There is no pretense, Lady Hazlet. I love your nephew."

"You dare to confuse lust with love? Everyone knows that witches aren't capable of love. Except perhaps with their own kind."

As Hazlet started to sweep past, Kylia got to her feet and stood in her way. "There is something I must tell you."

"I have no interest in anything you might want to say."

Kylia's voice lowered with feeling. "When first I arrived here, I was visited with a dream. In it I saw your brother and his friend on the field of battle. I watched them die, and heard their dying words." She saw the veiled head come up, and though she couldn't see Hazlet's eyes, she heard her suck in a breath.

Gathering her courage, she spoke quickly, before the woman could run. "Stirling and Ranald fought with great courage, but they were badly outnumbered."

"You could have learned that from anyone here at the castle. It was well known that my brother was headstrong. Even though he knew the Highlanders' strength was no match for the invaders, he used his charm to persuade his army to meet them on the field of battle. It was my brother's pride that caused the death of all those fine men, and the man I loved."

"Though you cast blame, Ranald never did. As he lay in Stirling's arms, breathing his last, he spoke only of you."

Hazlet went very still.

"Ranald begged your brother to watch out for you. He expressed fear that you would withdraw from the world. 'In fear and shame,' he said. And then his last words were that he loved you more than life itself."

If Kylia had expected her words to comfort the older woman, she was astounded when, instead of gratitude, Hazlet flew into a black, blinding rage.

"Witchcraft." The insult was torn from her lips while she lifted her hands to her ears, to block any further words Kylia might try to speak. "All of this is evil witchcraft, descended upon me by the devil himself."

"I thought…"

"You thought to trick me. To win my confidence, and then to betray me to the others. But I know your kind. Evil, evil witch." Hazlet pointed a finger at the wolf pup that, having heard her shouts, chewed nervously at the hem of Kylia's gown. "You belong together. Both creatures of the wild."

Lifting her skirts, Hazlet turned and began to run toward the castle, leaving Kylia to stare after her in amazement.

What had just happened here? What had caused this blazing anger?

As she went over in her mind what she'd said and done, Kylia could think of no reason for Hazlet's fury. She had simply affirmed that the man Hazlet loved above all others had returned that love, and had asked his best friend to watch out for her.

Lest she withdraw in shame and fear.

What did Hazlet have to fear after the death of her lover, except loneliness?

What would shame her, except her brother's headstrong actions that had taken him and his men into a battle they couldn't win? Yet Grant and Dougal felt nothing but pride at their father's courage.

How could the love of a good man, who returned that love, bring a woman shame and fear?

Kylia sank down onto the stone bench, hearing in her mind her grandmother's wise words. *Sometimes the answers to our questions are right before our eyes. All we need do is see things in a different light.*

As she lifted Wee Lad onto her lap and began

to soothe him, she pondered. What was she
missing? Who held the key to Hazlet's grief and
anger? And was this somehow connected to the
reason she had accompanied Grant to his world?

Chapter Sixteen

The evening meal in the great hall was once again attended by dozens of men, this time without their ladies. In what Kylia considered an ominous gesture, they wore the garb of warriors, their plaids tossed over one shoulder, swords in their scabbards, the hilts of dirks glinting at their waists.

As she moved among them, Kylia felt dwarfed by these tall, brawny Highlanders, so fierce, so solemn. She knew that the Council had been meeting behind closed doors for most of the day, and the sight of these intense faces had her heart beating overtime.

Grant looked equally intense as he escorted her to the table. She was relieved to see Hazlet already there, seated between Culver and Lord Giles. But was this a good thing, or did it signify that the older woman knew something the others didn't? With her veil in place, it was impossible to tell if she was grim or jubilant.

After showing Kylia to her seat, Grant rounded the table and caught Hazlet's hand, lifting it to his lips. "I bid you welcome, Aunt."

"I need not be welcomed in my own home." Hazlet neither smiled nor looked directly at him, keeping her gaze lowered behind her veil.

"True enough. But I'm grateful for the comfort of your presence at my table."

At a signal from Grant, the housekeeper ordered the wenches to begin serving. Dougal settled himself beside Kylia and, as always, began his joyful ritual of eating everything offered to him.

Seeing Kylia's smile, he paused to lick his fingers. "What do you eat in your kingdom, my lady?"

"We eat much the same as you. Fish. Fowl. Meat. And the many fruits and vegetables which we grow in our garden."

"You have a garden? Who tends it?"

"My sister Allegra loved it the most. But when she left to wed her Highland lord, the task fell to me, though occasionally my sister Gwenellen lends a hand."

"Can't you merely order the plants to grow?"

Kylia laughed. "Will you be greatly disappointed to learn that we must work, the same as you?"

He considered that a moment, before helping himself to a portion of salmon. "Aye, I confess to disappointment. I'd hoped your Mystical Kingdom was filled with all sorts of unbelievable things, like—" he paused to let his imagination soar "—fish that leap into your kettle, and birds that can talk."

Grant winked at Kylia before saying to his brother, "I suppose next you'll be wanting horses that fly, and tiny winged fairies that play among the trees?"

Those seated around the table burst into laughter, and Dougal looked sheepish for a moment before joining in. "I suppose I was being foolish. But what is the purpose of the Mystical Kingdom if it's just...ordinary?"

"Aye. What purpose indeed?" Grant shared a knowing smile with Kylia before sipping his ale.

"My laird." Seeing that the others had finished their meal, Giles got to his feet and took his sword from its scabbard, lifting it high in the air to signal silence.

Around the great hall, the crowd of warriors went silent, and the servants paused to watch and listen, for they sensed that this was a moment of great importance.

"This day the Council met to report on the condition of its citizens, and to discuss he who will lead us in the days to come." Giles turned to Culver, seated beside Hazlet. "Our esteemed cousin will announce the Council's decision."

Culver got to his feet and stepped away from the table so that his voice would carry over the length of the hall. "During the absence of our laird, Grant MacCallum, there were several sheep stolen from Kenneth MacCallum's flock. After the theft of the sheep, it was suggested that a new laird should be chosen, so that such a crime wouldn't be allowed to happen again." At a roar of voices raised in protest, Culver flushed. "It matters not who made this suggestion, but the name offered as laird was Dougal MacCallum, younger brother of our laird.''

Grant turned to study his brother, who was flushed with discomfort.

''Dougal rejected the offer and asked that the Council delay a decision until the return of his brother. When it was pointed out that the laird might never return from his dangerous journey, his brother became insistent that the Council bide its time.''

Culver waited until the hum of voices faded. ''It was later learned that the sheep were taken by a passing barbarian acting alone, who bartered them to James MacCallum for a blanket and a knife. When James learned of the theft, he returned the sheep to his cousin Kenneth.''

Culver cleared his throat. ''There was thought to be another crime while the laird was absent. The wee son of Russell MacCallum was missing for a day and feared kidnapped. Again it was suggested that our people were lacking a strong laird, but before action could be taken on the matter, it was discovered that the wee lad had been saved from drowning by the quick thinking of John MacCallum, who took the lad to his own home and fed and warmed him before returning him to his grateful parents.''

Culver looked around, pleased at the smiles creasing the faces of his kinsmen. Satisfied with his report, Culver turned to Giles, who walked over to stand beside him.

In a loud, clear voice Giles announced, ''Last evening we learned of the noble gesture by our laird that resulted in a pledge of loyalty from the leader of the clan Kerr. That only confirmed our faith in the man we chose to be laird. After a vote of all its members, this day the Council has once again affirmed its pledge of love and loyalty to our laird, Grant MacCallum.''

At that, Dougal removed his sword from his scabbard and presented it to his brother before kneeling at his feet to proclaim, ''To you, my brother and laird, I pledge my heart and my sword.''

Grant looked both astonished and pleased before touching the sword to Dougal's shoulder.

''Arise, my brother. Your devotion to me has touched me deeply.''

His words brought a mist of tears to Kylia's eyes, for she knew that, throughout Culver's long narrative, her worst fears had surfaced. How much greater it must have been for Grant.

Dougal was followed by Finlay, then by Giles, and finally by Culver, who knelt and swore their loyalty before being touched by their laird.

Afterward, every man in the room followed suit, walking to the laird's table, kneeling and swearing an oath of loyalty before stepping aside, until Grant was completely surrounded by his loyal warriors.

Kylia stared into the eyes of each man, hoping to spot one among them who might prove to be lying. But when all had gathered around their laird, she was no closer to the truth than before. Not a single man revealed himself to be the traitor.

She glanced at Hazlet, who had been quiet throughout the meal. The older woman seemed distracted, as though completely disinterested in this display of loyalty to her nephew. When she became aware that Kylia was watching, her agitation grew and she pushed away from the table before slipping away.

Her departure left Kylia deeply troubled.

* * *

"You're sure you saw no traitor among my men, my love?" Grant and Kylia lay in her pallet, watching as dark clouds scudded across the moon outside her balcony window.

"I searched their eyes. I saw nothing that spoke of betrayal."

"Could they hide such a thing from you?"

Kylia smiled and touched a finger to his mouth. Such a warm, firm mouth. It brought her so much pleasure. "Were you able to hide your feelings of love from me, my lord?"

That had him chuckling. "And I foolishly believed my thoughts were secret."

"So they are. Though you can't hide them from me—" she laughed "—I share them with no one else."

"Vixen." He drew her close and kissed her.

She leaned up, her hand on his chest. "Your heart should feel much lighter now that your men have pledged their love and loyalty to you."

"Aye." He leaned back, loving the feel of her fingers moving over him. "But I can't forget that someone close to me betrayed me before our last battle. I didn't imagine that, Kylia.''

Her hand stilled, for the same thought haunted her. ''I know.''

He spoke as though to himself. ''The MacCallum land is vast. Our people are scattered over hills and valleys. Many of my most trusted warriors have already returned to their homes to see to their flocks and crops. If I must, I'll have you accompany me as I visit every cottage and farm, until you've looked into the eyes of every last one.''

''If that is what you wish, my love.'' Though in truth, she knew of one right here in the castle whose eyes she had never seen. She hated to harbor such doubts about the very woman Grant considered a mother. But Hazlet's veil was the perfect foil for barring anyone seeing into her soul. Still Kylia was reluctant to make mention of her suspicions until she could confirm or deny them.

Grant nodded. ''Let me think on it.'' He drew her down. ''But for now, let me love you, my lady.''

Her humorous words were muffled against his mouth. ''If that is what you wish, my...''

The rest was swallowed by his kiss. And then there was no need for words as they lost themselves in their love.

Kylia stood on her balcony and watched as Grant and Dougal, accompanied by the ever-present Finlay, rode toward the village of Duncrune, where they had agreed to meet with Culver and Lord Giles.

Feeling restless, she drew a shawl around her shoulders before taking leave of her chambers, with Wee Lad at her feet. She would search the gardens for Hazlet, and try to find a way to see past the veil into the woman's soul. For, though it pained her greatly, she was becoming convinced that Grant's aunt was the key to his betrayal.

As Kylia started toward the garden she was stopped by Grant's housekeeper—tiny, birdlike Mistress Gunn.

"Are ye in need of something, my lady?"

It was the first time she could recall the old woman speaking directly to her. Perhaps Ardis had convinced her that she wouldn't be turned into a toad if she got too close to the witch. The thought of it had Kylia smiling, for she'd seen how most of the household staff kept their distance. "Nay, thank you. Since the lord is away, I thought I would walk in the garden. That is, if you have no objection, Mistress Gunn."

"None, my lady." The housekeeper eyed the wolf pup with suspicion. "But see ye keep your shawl tight around ye, for there's a bit of chill in the breeze this day." The old woman gave her a sideways glance. "Or do ye never feel the cold the way we do?"

"I feel all the things you feel, Mistress. Cold, hunger, fear."

"Fear?" The old woman's eyes widened. "Truly?"

"Truly. My sisters and I are ordinary women with some...extraordinary gifts which we are pledged to use only for good."

"So, ye wouldn't put a spell on someone in jest?"

"To do so would weaken our gifts. In time they could be lost to us, as they were lost to so many who came before us."

The housekeeper let out a long, slow sigh. "That's a comfort."

"Mistress Gunn, have you known the lady Hazlet all her life?"

"Aye, for I was at her mother's side for the birthing."

Seeing the pup chewing on the housekeeper's hem, Kylia picked him up and cuddled him in her arms. "As a lass, was she always so...stern?"

"Stern?" The old woman laughed. "Hazlet was a challenge to her parents. A wild one, that. Defied them at every turn. And defied her brother, Stirling, as well. She actually wanted to go with him and train to be a warrior."

"A warrior? Hazlet?" Kylia couldn't hide her surprise.

Mistress Gunn shook her head. "Everything changed after Ranald arrived. Young Hazlet found herself enjoying the womanly things she'd long denied. But when Ranald died, the lady took to her chambers, locking everyone out, and I fear she would have remained there until death claimed her, had it not been for Dougal's untimely birth."

"Did you attend that birthing as well?"

The old woman thought a moment. "It was

a difficult time in the castle. The small army of men left here to protect the women and children fought off the barbarians, and then began returning the bodies of the dead—'' she crossed herself ''—including the laird's body and that of Ranald. As I recall, Hazlet took charge of the birthing while we tended to the burials. It wasn't until later that we learned the lady Mary had died in childbirth.''

''And Hazlet never returned to her chambers?''

''How could she? There was the care of the bairn and his wee brother. And for a time, Hazlet seemed able to set aside her grief. But later, as the lads grew to manhood, the grief was back, and with it, a religious fervor the likes of which we'd never seen in the lady before.''

Seeing the cook waddling toward her, the housekeeper opened the door leading to the garden. ''Enjoy your walk, my lady.''

''Thank you, Mistress Gunn.'' Kylia slipped outside and set down the pup before starting along the garden path.

Because of the tall hedgerows, it was impossible to see from one pathway to another. Kylia drank in the beauty of her surroundings as she slowly made her way through the maze, pondering over all she'd been told.

At the sound of hoofbeats, she looked up to see Gresham, the stable master, leading one of the horses. At once Wee Lad raced to Kylia's side and huddled beneath the hem of her gown.

In a courtly gesture Gresham whipped the hat from his head and bowed. "Good day to you, my lady. Have ye been enjoying the gardens?"

"Aye. They're lovely." She glanced around. "I was hoping to share my walk with the lady Hazlet, but I saw no sign of her."

"If she's not in the gardens, then perhaps she's at the tombs. She visits daily, though it brings her no comfort." His voice lowered respectfully. "I fear the lady will never find peace until she joins Ranald in that other world."

"You think she desires death?"

The old man gave an expressive shrug of his shoulders. "I know not, my lady. But this much I know. She finds no pleasure in this life." He seemed about to say more, but thought better of it and simply said, "Would you like one of the servants to take you to the tombs?"

Kylia shook her head. "I'm told they lie beneath the castle."

"They do. If you go, take a candle, my lady, for it's dark and infested with all manner of vermin."

His words sent a shiver along Kylia's spine as she turned away.

Chapter Seventeen

With Wee Lad safely locked in her chambers, Kylia made her way down the narrow stone steps beneath the chapel. As she held her candle aloft she could see rodents scurrying across the dirt floor below. Above her head were rough-hewn timbers resting on columns of boulders that supported the structure.

She'd already begun to regret her decision to come here. It would be far wiser to wait until the morrow, when she could confront Hazlet in the sunny garden. Or perhaps she could persuade Ardis to take her to Hazlet's chambers, where the two women could converse in private. It would be much more civilized.

If she continued on this course of action, she

would have to deal with not only her suspicion, but the gloom and darkness of a catacomb. It was too daunting to contemplate. She was by nature a sunny person. She would prefer to deal with Hazlet in the light of day.

As she turned to retrace her steps, she heard a sound that had her stopping in her tracks. A woman's voice, moaning.

Had Hazlet fallen? If so, she would be lying hurt and alone in this horrid place. Despite her reluctance, Kylia's tender heart wouldn't permit her to flee. Turning back, she descended the last of the steps and followed the sound along a dark, narrow passageway. As she rounded a curve, she paused to stare at the scene before her.

Massive stone doors had been thrown wide, the timber used to secure them tossed to one side. Kylia stepped into a room that served as a family burial vault with perhaps a dozen crypts hewn of stone, resting above ground on stone pedestals. An ornately carved angel, arms aloft in welcome, stood guard in the center of the room. The flickering light of several torches thrust into niches in the walls sent eerie shadows dancing across the ceiling.

"My lady. Where are you? Are you hurt?" Kylia crossed the room, searching for the source of the cry.

She spotted Hazlet, who had flung herself across one of the crypts and lay, arms splayed as though trying to embrace the one buried within. Great choking sobs were torn from her throat.

Not hurt. Awash in grief.

Stunned by the depth of Hazlet's grief, Kylia turned away, ashamed of herself for intruding on such an intimate scene.

Before she could withdraw, Hazlet lifted her head and fixed Kylia with a look of fury. In a flash she was on her feet, charging across the room like some wild creature.

"By what right did you come here to my family home, thinking to offer me the comfort of my lover's last words? You had no such right, witch." She shoved Kylia hard enough to send her falling against the stone angel, where the candle slipped from her hand and dropped, sputtering in the dirt. As Kylia hit her head against the stone base, she saw a shower of stars dancing before her eyes.

It took a moment to catch her breath over the pain that was crashing through her. A thin line of blood trickled from her temple, staining her neckline and shoulder of her gown.

Thunderstruck at the violence of her actions, Hazlet stood over her, her hand to her mouth, her chest rising and falling with each labored breath. "Forgive me. I didn't mean to..." She sounded thoroughly confused. "I only meant to convey my anger. I never meant to..." She stooped down. "You're bleeding."

Kylia gave a hiss of pain and sat up slowly, waiting for the room to stop spinning. She sucked in a breath and struggled to put her thoughts into words. "This makes no sense. Why wouldn't it comfort you to know that Ranald's last coherent thought before giving up his life was of you, Lady Hazlet?"

"I had no need of reassurance." Hazlet backed away and began to pace, as though debating whether to run or remain. "I'd already had proof that he loved me."

Confused, still reeling, Kylia pulled herself up and staggered, falling against the crypt Hazlet had been embracing. In the flickering light of a torch, she caught sight of the name carved on the crypt.

It bore the name of Stirling MacCallum.

As the letters danced in front of Kylia's eyes, she shook her head and struggled to focus. Why Stirling? Why not Ranald?

"I don't understand. I thought your grief was for Ranald, the great love of your life. Why do you weep over your brother?"

Suddenly defiant, Hazlet lifted her chin. "This is none of your affair. Perhaps I weep for lost lives. Lost dreams. Whatever the reasons, they are mine, and mine alone. I need no witch to look into my soul."

"True enough. But what of the one who will judge you upon your death? Will you lie to heaven as well?"

"You would dare speak to me of heaven, when wicked souls like yours are condemned to hell for eternity?"

"Is that what you truly believe, Hazlet? Or is it merely what you want to tell yourself, for comfort?"

"I need no comfort. Not from the likes of you, nor from the things of this world."

Kylia looked around wildly for a chance to escape, for she was convinced this woman was mad. Seeing that Hazlet was blocking her way, she realized that she needed a weapon with which to defend herself. With a flash of insight, it came to her. Though this was neither the time nor the place, she needed to uncover Hazlet's secrets. They were the only weapons she needed.

Without warning, Kylia reached out and snatched the veil from Hazlet's face. Quick as a flash she dropped to the floor.

"How dare you…?"

Rolling aside, Kylia pulled herself up along the rough stone wall and closed her hand around one of the torches that had been thrust into a niche. Holding it aloft, she stared into Hazlet's icy eyes.

As their gazes locked, Kylia felt a jolt through her system. It was as though a dagger had been driven through her heart, sending her staggering backward until she came up against the cold stone of the crypt.

Seeing her pallor, Hazlet drew back and lifted a hand to shield her eyes from the light. "Nay. You'll not work your witchcraft on me."

"It's too late." Kylia's tone was without inflection as she lowered the torch and allowed it to be snuffed in the dirt.

There was no joy in the knowledge she'd gained. In the space of a heartbeat she'd seen it all. The love. The hate. The reason for the shame. And the desperation of a woman in conflict with all she believed.

Alarmed at Kylia's quiet resignation, Hazlet realized the worst. Could it be that this young woman was truly able to see into her soul?

She caught Kylia's arm, her voice a desperate plea. "You cannot tell. You must not. Don't you see? It will destroy us all."

"Aye." Kylia sank to her knees, too weak to stand.

Seeing it, Hazlet dropped to her knees beside her. "You'll keep my secret?"

Kylia looked up and once again found herself sinking into the woman's soul. She closed her eyes, wishing with every fiber of her being that she could erase all that she'd learned.

"I will not offer the truth. But if asked, I cannot lie. It is forbidden. For to do so, I would forfeit my gifts."

"Your gifts? Is this all you can think of? What about the lives of all those who will be destroyed by the truth?"

"The choice was yours, Hazlet. All those years ago, you chose a lie. And that lie has been eating at your soul ever since."

"What of it? It's my soul. My life. You have no right to it."

"That's so, my lady. And I wish to heaven I'd never heard of you or learned your lie. But I'm here at the request of your nephew, who loves you like a mother." The words had her covering her eyes with her hands to blot out the hideous irony. "And I'll not add to your lie with one of my own."

"You'll destroy us all." Hazlet snatched up a heavy golden candlestick and scrambled to her feet. "You think yourself better than mortals, do you, witch? A lot of good your honesty will do you now. You've just sealed your own fate."

"Would you add murder to your sins, Hazlet?"

At Kylia's words the older woman stared at her for long, silent moments before tossing the candlestick aside.

"If I can't kill you, I'll at least make you suffer, as I've suffered."

Like a madwoman, Hazlet raced about the room, snatching torches and candles, snuffing them into the dirt.

Holding the last remaining candle aloft, she made her way to the door and turned with a look of triumph.

"I can't think of a more perfect place for an other worldly creature than this room filled with the dead. Let's just see what powers you hold over them, witch."

Kylia watched as the doors slowly closed behind Hazlet, leaving the room in inky blackness. From beyond the doors, she could hear the sound of the timber being thrown into place to secure them.

Then there was an eerie silence broken only by the sound of her own shallow breathing, as Kylia struggled not to give in to the fear that threatened to engulf her. But as the silence deepened, she could hear the rustle of rodents slithering across the sand, and she stifled a scream as something brushed the hem of her gown.

* * *

"My lady?" Grant stepped into Kylia's chambers and was pounced upon by Wee Lad. With a laugh he cradled the little wolf in his arms and scratched behind his ear. "I can see that you're no longer the weak, wounded pup we found in the forest."

Grant looked over at the serving wench. "Ardis, would you fetch the lady from her sleeping chambers?"

"The lady Kylia isn't here, my lord."

He handed her the pup before turning away. "I'll find her below stairs."

After walking the length of the gardens and back, he went in search of the housekeeper. He found her in the great hall, preparing a tray of ale for their dinner.

When she looked up, he said, "I thought I'd find the lady Kylia here with you."

"Nay, my lord. I haven't seen the lady since early this afternoon." Seeing Dougal just entering the hall with Hazlet, she smiled. "Shall I serve your evening meal now, my lord?"

"Not until I find the lady Kylia."

Hearing him, Dougal laughed. "Is she lost, or merely hiding?"

Grant shrugged. "Her servant hasn't seen her, nor has Mistress Gunn, since this afternoon."

"Perhaps she went to the village."

Grant shook his head. "We would have passed her along the way." He started out. "I'll inquire of the servants. Someone must have seen her."

Dougal turned to follow. "I'll walk to the stable. Perhaps she decided to ride."

Distracted, Grant merely nodded. "If so, Gresham would know."

When they were gone, Hazlet walked to the fire to warm herself. She looked every inch the proper mistress of Duncrune Castle. She had changed into a fresh gown and headdress, her hair tucked out of sight, her veil in place to screen her face. But she was so cold. Not even the logs blazing on the hearth could chase the chill from her soul. It was as though her blood had turned to ice.

Or perhaps, she thought with a shudder, it was her heart that had frozen.

For so long now she had gone through the motions of living. But her life had ended that day on the field of battle, when her brother, and then her lover, had given up their lives.

And now she felt as though it were all happening again. The pain, the shock, the fear and shame.

All because of the witch.

Chapter Eighteen

Kylia took deep, calming breaths until the first frantic feeling of panic passed. What was there to fear, after all? Hazlet hadn't harmed her. She had merely locked her in the burial vault. Though it was dark and damp and chilly, it posed no threat to her life. She had suffered discomfort before. She drew her shawl more tightly around her shoulders and began sorting through her dilemma. The first thing she needed was light.

She extended her arms and began to chant the ancient words. Within minutes there was a faint glow of light. She looked over and saw a torch lying in the dirt, with a fire just beginning to burn at the tip. With a feeling of elation, she raced across the room and held the torch aloft until it was ablaze. After thrusting it into a niche in the wall she retrieved the other torches and candles and held them to the flame until they, too, were ablaze.

She stood in the middle of the room and experienced a wave of confidence. She now had heat and light.

Just then a fat mouse scampered across the toe of her boot. Although her first inclination was to cringe, she forced herself to stoop down and hold out a hand. "Hello, little creature. Am I intruding on your home?"

The mouse stopped, sniffed her fingers and stood on its hind legs.

"Let me see if I have any crumbs from Wee Lad's meal." She reached into a pocket of her gown and withdrew a tiny morsel of the biscuit she'd shared with her pup hours earlier.

When she held out her hand, the mouse eyed her suspiciously before moving closer. At last, too hungry to resist, it stepped into her palm and devoured the food.

"You see?" She laughed. "I was afraid of you, and you were afraid of me. But here we are, sharing your home and my food. Now, if only you were strong enough to lift the latch that is keeping me prisoner.''

When the mouse scurried away, Kylia turned to the door and decided to try another spell. Perhaps the one Gwenellen had once used to lift Bessie all the way to the roof of their cottage. How they'd laughed at the look on poor Bessie's face. Of course, Gwenellen had been trying to make it rain. Poor thing. She did have a bad time of it with spells.

Holding her arms aloft, Kylia began to chant the ancient words. Moments later she heard the scrape of the heavy timber being lifted from the latch. As the doors opened, she turned with a smile.

But it hadn't been her chanting that had opened the door. It was Hazlet, standing in the doorway, holding in her hand a very small, very menacing knife.

''Grant.'' Dougal burst into the house, followed by the stable master. ''Gresham told me that Kylia planned to join our aunt in the burial chambers.''

Grant turned, holding Wee Lad in his arms. "It's odd that Aunt Hazlet never mentioned it."

"It was hours ago, my lord." Gresham pulled the hat from his head in a gesture of respect. "The lady Hazlet may have forgotten by now."

"Aye." Dougal eyed the wolf pup. "Why not turn Kylia's lap dog loose to find her?"

Grant thought about it a moment before nodding. "Why not indeed? He dotes on her and she on him." He lowered the pup to the floor and said, "Find your mistress, Wee Lad."

The pup stood a moment, looking around in confusion. Then it bounded across the floor and headed toward the chapel, with Grant and Dougal following. Once there, the pup sniffed the stone steps before starting down, with the two men close on his heels.

As they made their way into the dank bowels of the castle, Dougal sighed. "I can't imagine the lady Kylia venturing into such a place."

"Nor I." Grant was frowning as the pup raced ahead. "Had I known our aunt was spending her time in such as this, I'd have forbidden her to return. No wonder her spirits have been so low these many years. Just seeing this place has me yearning to breathe fresh air and see the light of morning.''

As they progressed along a dark hallway, they could see flickering light up ahead, and could hear the sound of feminine voices. Recognizing Hazlet's, they paused to listen.

''It was wrong of me to lock you in here, Kylia Drummond. You did nothing to deserve such treatment.'' Hazlet stopped speaking to look around, as the realization dawned. ''I left you with no light, and yet the torches now burn. How is this possible?''

Kylia's voice held no trace of anger or bitterness. ''It is just one of the many gifts I've discovered, though in truth, I'm not certain if I could recall the proper words.''

''You...conjured up the light?''

''I was trying to lift the latch as well, and actually thought I had, when the doors opened. Alas, I see that my meager gifts apparently don't run to such as that. But I'm grateful that you came back to free me, Hazlet.''

Spying Grant and Dougal in the doorway, she smiled a greeting. ''How did you find me? Did your aunt bring you?''

There was no answering smile from Grant. He looked from Kylia to his aunt. "What is the meaning of this? Did I hear correctly? Did you lock Kylia in this dismal place?"

Hazlet's lips turned into a scowl. "What transpired here was between the two of us. I've no intention of discussing it with you, nephew." She started away, tucking the knife into the pocket of her coarse gown. At the door she turned. "I'm certain the witch will be happy to tell you everything. It's why she's here, after all."

As the sound of her footsteps faded, Grant turned to Kylia. "My aunt spoke about locking you in this place. Is this true?"

Kylia looked from Grant to Dougal, seeing the same puzzled looks on both their faces. "Your aunt was vexed, and did something she now regrets. I must accept her apology and bear her no ill will."

Dougal's lips split into a smile. "By heaven, I see now why my brother loves you so. You're a remarkable woman, Kylia."

Instead of feeling joy at his words, she felt her heart sink. "We mustn't speak of love now."

Grant was watching her closely. "I agree. There will be time for that later. For now, tell me what transpired between you and my aunt that she would lock you away in this dreary place."

Kylia shook her head and studied the toe of her kid boot. "I cannot tell you that."

Grant strode closer and caught her chin in his hand, forcing her to meet his eyes. "You will tell me."

"Nay." She saw the range of emotions caused by her denial of his request. Pain. Anger. Puzzlement.

"Tell me the truth, Kylia. Have you learned something that is vital to me?"

"I have. But it is Hazlet's secret, and only she can reveal it." She took a step back, breaking contact. "I wish to return to my kingdom."

His eyes narrowed. "We had an agreement. You would stay until you learned the name of the one who betrayed…" His words died as the realization dawned. For long moments he studied her before saying, "I will deal with this, and then we'll speak of your future."

Kylia shook her head. "I'd hoped…" The

thought of her shattered hopes and dreams caused a pain around her heart like no other. But she knew that she could no longer remain here, knowing the secrets in Hazlet's heart. "I must leave here, Grant. I cannot stay."

His voice lowered with feeling. "Please, my lady. It isn't possible for me to leave my people at this perilous time. I must see this thing with my aunt through to its conclusion."

"And I must leave, for my presence here will only be the source of pain for you and for her."

While Dougal glanced from one to the other, the silence stretched between them.

Finally Grant gave a slight nod of his head. "Very well. I'll send my most trusted man, Finlay, to accompany you."

"Let me go, too, Grant." Dougal turned a pleading look on his brother. "It would be an honor for me to accompany the lady to her kingdom."

Grant frowned. "Not to mention an adventure."

"Aye. One I've long dreamed of."

"Beware, Dougal. The journey isn't a pleasant one. You'll be sorely tested, both in body and in mind."

Dougal stiffened his spine. "Do you think me less a warrior than Finlay?"

"Of course not." Grant clapped a hand on his brother's shoulder and drew him close. "But there are many who attempted to reach the Mystical Kingdom and didn't live to tell of it. I love you, Dougal. You are all the family I have."

"I'll make you proud." The younger man stepped back and gave his brother a radiant smile. "Then you and I will sit around the fire in our old age and talk of the wondrous things we saw in the lady's kingdom."

Kylia's voice had him looking up. "You misunderstand, Dougal. You will be permitted to escort me only to the edge of the Enchanted Loch. From there, I will return alone to my kingdom."

"Why must I stop at the banks of the loch?"

"There are forces that will prevent you from going on."

"My brother overcame the forces."

Kylia felt a pain at the memory. "Aye, Dougal. There was a fire burning in your brother's heart that was strong enough to overcome the forces. No such fire burns in your heart." She thought of Hazlet's secrets. "At least not now. But perhaps one day."

Grant turned to Dougal. "Do you still wish to accompany the lady?"

The younger man nodded. "Aye. For I'll still get to experience the Forest of Darkness, and see the waters of the Enchanted Loch."

"Very well then. Go and prepare to leave on the morrow."

When Dougal hurried away, Grant caught Kylia's hands in his and drew her close. "I must speak with Finlay and arrange for some of my men to accompany him. After that, I'll come to you in your chambers."

She sighed. "To bid me goodbye?"

"To try to change your mind, my love. For if you leave me, my heart will surely stop beating."

"As will mine. But it must be done."

He stopped her words with a hard, quick kiss. Then, gathering her into his arms, he kissed her again until they were both dazed and clinging.

He pressed his forehead to hers. "How can I bear to let you go, Kylia?"

"No more than I can bear to leave you. But I must."

He took her hand, linking her fingers with his. At the doorway he stooped to pick up the wolf pup before handing it over to Kylia.

In silence they climbed the steps, knowing that each one brought them closer to the pain of parting.

Chapter Nineteen

While Grant stood talking quietly with Finlay and Dougal, Kylia stood before the blazing fire in the great hall, cradling Wee Lad in her arms. Neither the warmth of the pup nor the fire could chase the chill that had settled around her heart.

She loved Grant. And she'd come to love his home and people, as well. But how could she stay here, knowing the secret Hazlet harbored in her heart? Such a thing would eat away at the love she and Grant shared. He would resent the fact that she knew something she refused to share with him. And in time it would destroy whatever feelings they had for each other.

She heard Grant's voice, low, resigned. "It's settled then. You'll leave on the morrow."

Kylia pressed her face to the pup's neck, wishing she could give in to the need to weep.

"My laird." Ardis came rushing into the great hall and nearly collided with Mistress Gunn, who was just passing around a tray of goblets filled with ale.

"Have ye no manners, wench?" The old housekeeper shot her a withering look. "Ye'll leave the laird's presence at once."

"But Mistress Gunn…" The girl struggled to catch her breath.

"Ye heard me. Out with ye."

Ardis turned away. In the doorway she muttered, "The lady Hazlet said I was to tell the laird…"

"Hazlet?" Grant set aside his goblet. "What about my aunt, Ardis?"

The lass looked from Mistress Gunn, who was scowling, to the lord, who beckoned her closer. Timidly she retraced her steps, wringing her hands together to calm her nerves.

"When the lady Hazlet learned that Dougal was leaving Duncrune Castle to escort the lady Kylia to her home, she became…highly agitated. She sent me to fetch you, my lord, along with your brother and the lady."

"To her chambers?"

Ardis shook her head. "Nay, my lord. To the burial vault."

Grant stepped away from the others and crossed to where Kylia stood alone. "You heard?"

She nodded.

He put a hand under her elbow. "Come, my love."

With Dougal on one side of her and Grant on the other, Kylia made her way once again toward the steps leading to the catacombs. With each step she could feel her heart thundering. Was Hazlet about to reveal her secret? If so, how would Grant and Dougal react to the news?

For Kylia, speaking the truth was as natural as breathing. But for someone like Hazlet, who had spent a lifetime in a lie, it might prove to be earth-shattering. It would surely bring pain to those who had innocently believed in her.

When they stepped into the burial vault, Hazlet was standing between the crypts of Stirling and Ranald. The flickering light from torches lining the wall gave her face an eerie quality of darkness and light.

"Hold." She lifted an arm, bidding them to stop some distance away. She ignored Kylia and Dougal, keeping her gaze fixed on Grant. "As a lass, I was jealous of my brother, Stirling. You're so like him. While he studied the ancient languages, I was taught needlework. But while I plied my lessons in silence, I listened and learned. When he went off to study with warriors, I remained behind, to learn the humble art of keeping house for a man. But in my heart I was as much a warrior as he. And when he returned to be proclaimed laird of our clan, I begged to be allowed to go with him to the field of battle."

"A warrior?" Grant shook his head. "I never knew, Aunt."

"How could you? It was my secret. And later, my shame."

"I don't…"

She lifted her hand for silence. "When Stirling returned home from his studies, he brought with him a cousin, Ranald, who had become his closest friend. Ranald was not like other warriors. There was a gentleness, a kindness in him that I'd never seen in another man. He genuinely cared what was in my mind and heart. We talked endlessly about everything. In time, I lost my heart to him. I was young and foolish, and wildly in love.'' She swallowed. ''When we learned that invaders were coming to our Highlands from two sides, it was agreed that Ranald would lead an army of warriors to the north, and Stirling would lead the rest to the south. A third army would remain here in the village, to protect those left behind.'' She paused to collect her thoughts. ''Something was happening to me that I couldn't understand. I wept for no reason. I sulked, even when Ranald tried to comfort me. And when I learned the reason for these changes, I became convinced that my brother would have me put away in a cloister, never to be seen again.''

''Why would you think such a thing, Aunt?''

At Dougal's question, she looked over at him, as though seeing him for the first time. Her eyes softened for a moment, before she blinked and looked away.

''I decided that I must act first, before my brother could succeed with such a deed. And so when he left with his army, I sent a missive to our attackers, letting them know where my brother would choose to defend our land.''

"You betrayed your own brother?'' Grant's voice cut like the blade of his sword, which he jerked from its scabbard, causing Hazlet to flinch.

"Aye.'' She lifted her head. "I'll blame you not for killing me in return. Death no longer holds any threat to me, for I have paid the price for my sin in ways worse than death.'' Her voice lowered as she continued her recitation. "I had no way of knowing that Stirling had changed his plans, and had asked Ranald to fight at his side. When I learned that both my brother and the man I loved were dead, I locked myself away, vowing to remain in my chambers alone until death took me, as well.''

"But you didn't die, Aunt.'' Grant took a step closer, holding his sword in a menacing gesture.

"I did. In ways you will never know or understand.'' She glanced at Kylia. "The witch knows what happened next, for she ripped my veil from my eyes and peered into my soul. And now, it matters not that you know, as well.'' She lifted her head proudly. "I was not hiding out of grief, but of shame. For I was carrying Ranald's babe.''

That had Grant and Dougal staring at each other in stunned surprise.

"What happened to the babe?'' Grant's tone hardened. "Did you kill it to spare yourself the guilt?''

"I suppose, in my dazed state, I contemplated it, though I never could have carried out such a horror against a helpless babe.''

"Why not? You've admitted causing your own brother's death.''

"Aye. But I hadn't truly thought about the consequences of my action. There was a demon inside me, causing me to behave in a manner that was foreign to anything I'd ever done before.''

Dougal stepped up to stand beside Grant. "What did you do with the babe, Aunt Hazlet?''

She looked away. "Your mother found her time coming too soon. Because of the battle being waged around the castle, there was no one else to assist. When Mary saw me, she knew at once that my own time had also come. In tears, I confessed my guilt and begged her forgiveness. I'll never know if it was the shock of learning that I had betrayed her husband, or the birth itself. Whatever the reason, both Mary and her infant died.''

"Nay.'' Dougal lifted a hand. "You mean our mother died. I am still here, Aunt.''

She looked at him then, and tears filled her eyes. "You are not Mary and Stirling's son, Dougal. You are my son. I knew that by passing you as theirs, you would be loved by our people, instead of being reviled by them as Ranald's bastard.''

In the silence that followed, she choked back a sob. "My punishment has been to watch you grow to manhood, without ever once hearing you call me mother.''

Grant's voice was low with fury. "Is this why you betrayed me, as you betrayed my father? So that Dougal could take my place as lord?''

She nodded, too overcome to speak. Finally she said in a whisper, "Do not blame Dougal, for he is innocent of this.''

"I do not blame him.'' Grant turned to the younger man. "He will always be the brother of my heart. As for you, Aunt…''

She shook her head. "There is a demon inside me. At times I can overcome it. At other times it overcomes me, and I give in to its voice." She looked up, allowing her gaze to move slowly over Grant. Then she turned and studied Dougal as though memorizing every line and feature of his face. "You're like him, you know. So like my beloved Ranald. Kind and patient and good. Forgive me, my son."

In one smooth motion she reached into the pocket of her gown and withdrew a dirk. The razor-sharp blade glinted in the light of the torches.

Before any of them could move, she lifted it high and plunged it into her chest, then threw herself onto her lover's crypt to die.

Dougal was the first to reach Hazlet's side, lifting her gently away from the crypt and lowering her to the floor, while blood spilled through his fingers and pooled around her.

"Help her." He cried to Kylia. "If anyone can save her, it's you, my lady."

"I wish it were so." Kylia knelt in the dirt beside him.

"You are a witch."

"Aye. But my gift of healing is weak. I would need my family around me to heal a wound as mortal as this."

"Then summon them, my lady. I beg of you."

Kylia looked to Grant, who stood over them, staring down at the woman he'd loved and honored for a lifetime.

He gave a grudging nod. "Aye, my lady. Dougal is right. We must do all we can to save her."

Kylia closed her eyes and extended her arms. "My family. A boon I would beg of thee. Leave the comfort of your home and come to me."

There was a roaring sound as though of a great wind. The light of the torches began swaying wildly. Suddenly in their midst stood three women in flowing robes. Each of them in turn greeted Kylia with an embrace.

"Mum. Gram. Gwenellen. I'm so glad you could come."

"How could we not?" Nola said gently.

Suddenly there was another rush of wind. When the light of the torches settled, a fourth young woman stood in their midst.

"Allegra. Oh, Allegra." The others gathered around to hug her fiercely.

"I was walking in the gardens with my beloved Merrick when I heard a voice summoning me. I fear my husband was a bit startled, but then," she added with a smile, "he's learned to expect the unexpected with a witch for a wife." She turned to Kylia. "Why did you summon me?"

"I need you, Allegra." Kylia turned to the others. "I need all of you. This is Hazlet, whose shame and guilt caused her to attempt to end her life."

Wilona gently probed the wound. "It is grave, indeed. Perhaps it is best if she be allowed to enter the other side."

"Nay." Dougal's cry had them turning to him.

"He has just learned that the woman he called aunt is really his mother." Kylia caught her sisters' hands. "Think of all the things in his heart that will never be spoken if she dies now."

The women looked around, then began to form a circle around Hazlet.

Wilona turned to Dougal and held out a hand. "You are blood of her blood. It is important for you to join the circle."

He took her hand in his.

Seeing Grant standing off to one side, Kylia held out a hand. "You, too, are blood of her blood, my love."

At her endearment, the other women looked at one another in surprise.

As Grant caught Kylia's hand, she stooped and picked up the wolf pup, tucking him into the front of Grant's tunic. Then, as the circle was completed, she nodded to her grandmother, who began to chant the ancient words. Gradually the others picked up the words, until the room was filled with the sound of their chanting.

Suddenly the room fell away. They were no longer in the vault but were soaring high in the sky, with Hazlet still lying in the middle of the circle.

Though Dougal's eyes rounded with amazement, he held tightly to the hands in his. Grant did the same, watching as Kylia and her family continued chanting the ancient words.

They floated over hills and meadows,

Highland lochs and streams, and dense forests, before settling in a verdant meadow filled with the fragrance of wildflowers.

As they continued holding hands and chanting the words, they saw Hazlet's eyelids flutter, then open.

"You're alive, Mother." Dougal dropped to his knees beside her, while the others watched in silence.

"Mother?" Hazlet sat up with a look of amazement. "Have I died and gone to heaven, then?"

"Nay. Kylia and her family brought you back."

"The witch?" She looked around at the others. "Am I here to be punished for my sins?"

"Nay," Wilona said gently. "You are returned so that you can have another chance to be the woman you were meant to be."

"And what is that?" Hazlet asked.

Dougal took her hand in his. "Perhaps you can start by being my mother."

She looked over at Grant. "And what of you, nephew? As laird, you have the right to have me put to death for my betrayal."

"I do. It's tempting, since my heart is heavy over the loss of the father I never knew. But how can I do less than Dougal? Or this woman, whose goodness puts us all to shame?"

Seeing Kylia standing beside Grant, a range of emotions crossed Hazlet's face. "I have been wicked. Cruel. Dishonest. All the things I accused you of, my lady. And yet you would use your gifts to save me? How can I ever make amends?"

Kylia smiled. "You can live the rest of your life in kindness and charity and honesty. For it is demanded of all who are brought back from that other life."

"I give you my word on it." Hazlet's eyes slowly closed.

Dougal looked up in alarm. "Is she slipping away again?"

"Nay." Wilona knelt beside him. "She has had a long and difficult journey from the other side. You must leave her to rest now. My daughter and I will see to her care." She turned to Gwenellen. "Perhaps you and the lad could explore our kingdom for a while."

"Aye." With a laugh Gwenellen caught

Dougal's hand and the two started off across the meadow.

Gwenellen paused to glance at her sister, still standing beside Grant. "Are you coming?"

Grant shook his head. "We'll stay here, for there is much we must speak of."

As Gwenellen and Dougal skipped away, Kylia caught the somber look in Grant's eyes and felt her heart stop. There was something dark and unfathomable about him now that frightened her more than the Forest of Darkness, or even the secrets she'd uncovered in Hazlet's heart.

Chapter Twenty

Kylia touched Grant's arm. "What is it, my love?"

He caught her hand and walked with her, until they came up over a hill in the meadow. Below them were Gwenellen and Dougal, looking up at the trees, where the fairies giggled and whispered. Across the meadow, outside their snug cottage stood Nola and Bessie, stirring something in a big kettle, preparing a meal, while Wilona and Jeremy knelt on either side of the prone figure of Hazlet, bathing her forehead, covering her with a fur throw.

Grant's tone was solemn and serious. "So much has happened. The things I've learned have shaken me to my core. I'm not the man I thought I was, nor is Dougal the brother I thought him to be.''

"But you still love each other. That hasn't changed.''

"Aye. I love him. But our loyalties will now be divided. I can see that he wants to know the mother he never had, while I resent her for depriving me of the father I never had.''

"Your resentment will fade in time, Grant.''

"I fervently pray it is so. I don't want to harbor hatred in my heart. Not when I see the goodness in you. But I don't know if I'm capable of the kind of forgiveness that will be necessary to heal our family.''

"It will take time.''

"Time.'' He said the word on a sigh of disgust.

"Aye. Give yourself time to let these changes merge with what once was. Time to forgive, to learn to love.''

"What if I can't? What if the fabric of our family is forever torn apart?''

"Then you'll weave a new one. We'll weave a new fabric together, and you'll see that none of the old ways matter.''

"But they matter to me, don't you see?" He studied their linked fingers, then slowly released his hold on her. "You live in paradise. I live in a world of lies and deception and violence. What man would want to share such horror with someone as good, as loving, as you?"

"But I've learned to love your land, your people."

"Aye. Because your heart is so good and pure. But don't you understand, Kylia? The people of my world will never change. Even those who proclaim themselves holy will cheat and lie and steal." His voice lowered with feeling. "And kill. Look at me. I've killed men on the field of battle. What is the difference if we kill our enemies, or our brothers?"

"It does matter, Grant." She touched her hands to his face and stared into his eyes, willing him to see the truth of her words. "You fight the invaders in order for your people to live in peace. You're even willing to sacrifice your life for theirs. Can anything be more honorable than that?"

"It may be necessary, and honorable, but it will never be good to take another's life. While you and your family spend your time healing, I spend mine inflicting mortal wounds. How can I ask you to give up a life in paradise for such as I can offer?''

''Ask me.'' Though she tried to keep the plea from her tone, it was there. ''Just ask me, my lord, and let the choice be mine.''

Instead of the words she desperately wanted to hear, he merely shook his head and turned away, leaving her standing alone at the top of the hill, her heart shattering into millions of pieces.

They gathered around a festive table set beneath the shade of a tree. The contrast between Kylia and her family, in their lavish gowns the color of flowers seemed all the more distinct when measured against the dulness of Hazlet's nun's robes. Though she no longer wore the veil across her face, she had carefully tucked her hair under a length of brown cloth, and kept her head bowed while the others carried on a lively conversation. It was plain to all that guilt weighed heavily upon her.

Wilona draped an arm around her daughter

and glanced with affection at her three grand-daughters, who were taking turns feeding Wee Lad. "Isn't it grand to have them back with us?"

"Aye." Nola squeezed Allegra's hand. "How is life with your beloved Merrick and his son, Hamish?"

"We're so happy, despite the fact that Merrick was recently gone from us for more than a fortnight, leading an army against invaders."

Grant looked over at Kylia's older sister with sudden interest. "How do you survive the loss of your husband to battle, my lady?"

"Like any other wife, I stay as busy as I can while worrying over him."

"But it has to be worse for someone like you."

She arched a brow. "Someone like me?"

"Have you no regrets over giving up paradise for a mere mortal?"

Laughter lurked in her eyes, though she kept her voice without inflection. "Merrick may be a mortal, but there is nothing mere about him. Nor about the love I feel for him. What good would paradise do me without him in it?"

"What good?" He gave a mirthless laugh. "Here there is no cruelty. No sickness. No lying or cheating. Here you would still enjoy the love of your family. You could share laughter, and feel the warmth of sunshine on your face every day. There would be no pain, no sorrow."

"No sorrow? If you think that, you have never experienced love, my lord. I was warned that I would be changed by the love of a mortal. But until I experienced it for myself, I didn't understand. You think us different from mortals, but you're wrong. Once we have found love, we become like you. We can be lifted to the highest heavens by the sheer joy of loving. We can be dashed to the depths of despair by the loss of that love. You see, Grant MacCallum, despite all our gifts here in the Mystical Kingdom, all our strengths and spells, our hearts can be broken."

Nola glanced at Kylia, who had been strangely silent throughout the meal. "Come, my daughter. Help me serve the tea."

When they were inside the cottage, Nola arranged cups on a tray while Kylia poured from the kettle.

"Do you love this man, my child?"

"Aye." She said it simply.

"Yet the love makes you unhappy. Does he not return your feelings?"

"I believe he does. But the secrets revealed by his aunt have left him angry and bitter. He is reluctant to bring me into such a household."

Nola smiled. "He thinks others have a perfect family, and his is imperfect."

Kylia nodded.

Nola laid a hand over hers. "If you love him, and he returns that love, you will find a way."

"How?" Kylia's eyes filled with tears. "He is eager to return to his home. And he has made it plain that he will not ask me to accompany him."

Nola merely patted her daughter's hand. "Then you must find a way to change his mind. You are, after all, endowed with certain gifts."

"But you and Gram taught me that I have no right to use them for my own selfish needs."

"Perhaps, just this once, we could make an exception."

When her mother walked away carrying the tray, Kylia remained alone in the kitchen, staring after her. And wondering how in the world she could work her magic on such a stubborn, pigheaded man as Grant MacCallum.

As their little party sipped tea and ate fruit fresh from the trees, the sun sank beneath the hills, and the shadows of evening began to gather around them.

Hazlet, seated beside Dougal, turned to Kylia and broke her self-imposed silence. "My lady, how can I ever thank you and your family for the precious gift you gave me?"

"Your thanks are not necessary." Kylia glanced at her family, who nodded their agreement.

"But I wish to make amends for my sins." She studied her nephew's stern profile. "I allowed bitterness and pride and grief to ruin not only my life, but all those I loved. Please believe me when I tell you that I would gladly exchange this new life I've been given, if it would but convince you that the most important thing in this world is love. Not all of us find it. And some who do, discover that it is not returned. But if you are fortunate enough to love one who loves you in return, do all in your power to cherish it as the greatest gift of all.''

Abruptly Grant got to his feet and turned to the others at table. ''By your leave, I need to walk off this fine meal.''

As he started away, Kylia stood up. ''I believe I'll partake of this evening air as well.''

At once, the wolf pup danced at her heels.

The others remained by the cottage, watching as the two shadowy figures blended into the darkness.

Kylia moved slowly beside Grant, aware that he was taking great pains not to touch her. When they reached the top of the hill, they lifted their heads to stare at the canopy of stars above them.

''My sisters and I rode among them one night.''

He turned to study her. ''What was it like?''

''Breathtaking. Like…'' She struggled to find a way to describe it. ''Like the first time you kissed me.''

He felt a trickle of heat along his spine, remembering that first time, and the indelible effect it had on him. ''I doubt a kiss can compare with a ride among the stars.''

"It can, if the two sharing the kiss are fated to be together from the beginning of time."

"Kylia, you don't know…"

She turned and placed a finger to his lips to silence his protest. "I saw you when I was but a wee lass, and my heart knew you. After that, every time your face appeared in the loch, or in my dreams, I came to know you better. You can no more deny me than you can deny yourself, my love."

He caught her wrist. "My mind is made up, Kylia. When I leave this place, I leave alone."

"Because you feel unworthy of me." She said it softly, with no bitterness.

"Aye."

Her tone lowered with feeling. "If you leave without me, you will never know a moment's peace. I'll haunt your dreams, and stalk you as you go about your daily routine. You'll see my face on every maiden, and hear my voice in the ripple of a brook. With every breath you take, you'll breathe me in. And you'll mourn your loss as only a scorned lover can."

He was shocked by her fervor. "Such cruelty is beneath you, my lady."

"It will not be of my making, but of yours. You see how your aunt suffered for a lifetime because of the choices she made, and yet you consider making like choices."

"I choose not to lie or cheat in order to have what my heart desires. Can't you see that, Kylia? I could lie, and promise you paradise in my arms. It would be paradise for me, but for you it would mean a lifetime of hell, waiting while I battle yet another army of invaders. I could beg, and tell you that I will never love another the way I love you. And though it may be true, it is also selfish. I want better for you than what I can offer."

"And what about what I want?" When he didn't answer she gave a sigh. "I want you, Grant. Only you. And this." She wrapped her arms around his neck and stood on tiptoe to press her mouth to his. "Only this."

He'd thought he could resist. But the moment her mouth was on his, he felt the jolt of need, hot and demanding, and answered with a slow, deep kiss that had his head spinning, the ground beneath his feet tilting wildly.

Against her lips he murmured, "How could

you possibly want me, Kylia? I'm weak, my love.'' He drew back. ''A weak, mortal man. It's another thing you'll surely regret one day.''

''There will be no regrets.'' She drew herself against him, needing to feel him in every part of her body. ''Not now, not ever.''

''Oh, my love.'' He rained kisses over her eyes, her cheeks, the tip of her nose, before once more claiming her mouth. ''How did I ever live before you? Promise me, no matter how foolishly I behave, you'll never leave me.''

''I promise you.''

''And I promise you that I will love only you, my sweet, beautiful Kylia.'' He gathered her close and pressed his mouth to her temple, breathing her in.

Overhead, the stars began dancing across the sky in a glittering display of fireworks. At their feet, Wee Lad lifted his head to the moon and, for the first time in his young life, howled.

As the two of them drew a little apart, Grant said with a laugh, ''I see that here in the Mystical Kingdom you have some unusual ways of announcing things of importance.''

''Aye. I hope you don't mind.''

"Mind?" He chuckled, low and deep in his throat. "I thought about shouting it from the treetops. But your way is much better, my love."

He caught her hand, and with the wolf bounding at their feet, they turned back toward the cottage, to share their news with the others.

Epilogue

The little party stood in a circle, each of them holding a candle. The moon was a fat golden globe in the midnight sky. The night air was sweet with the scent of roses.

Dougal stood beside Grant, his hand on his shoulder, watching as Kylia, accompanied by her sisters Allegra and Gwenellen, stepped out of the cottage and began to cross the meadow toward them.

She wore a gown of white gossamer that could have been spun by angels. Her thick black hair, entwined with wildflowers, drifted about her face and shoulders like a silken veil.

When she reached Grant, he took her hands in his and was stunned not only by the heat of her touch, but by the look of love in her eyes.

A look so deep, so dazzling, it had his heart stuttering.

The two of them turned toward Wilona, who laid her hands over their joined hands.

"To all things there is a season. A time to live. A time to love."

Hearing the familiar words, Kylia felt tears sting her eyes.

"Speak now what is in your hearts."

Grant's voice was strong, rich, as he smiled down at his bride. "I'd thought I could deny my love for you, in order to spare you the hardships of my world. But I can no more deny you, my love, than I could deny my own life. I love you, Kylia, of the clan Drummond. I will cherish you for my lifetime, and beyond." He removed a small pouch from his tunic and opened it to reveal the jewels he'd once plucked from the Enchanted Loch. "With these stones I pledge my love and my life."

As they spilled into her hand, they seemed to flow like liquid tears, pale and luminous as the stars overhead. Then, while some mysteriously danced in her hair, others formed a circlet around her throat, held in place by nearly invisible strands of fine gold.

Kylia blinked away her tears, for she wanted

nothing to mar her view of this man's face, as she spoke from her heart. "I have known you for all of my life. My friend, my love, my husband. I will be with you forever, in this world and the next."

Wilona lifted her hands over their heads in a blessing. "Now you are no longer two, but one. One heart. One love. One will. You no longer have two families, but one. Go now, and make your life together. But remember always that you have a home here in the Mystical Kingdom. The ones you leave behind will be awaiting your visits."

They turned to accept the warm congratulations and embraces from their family.

Nola wiped tears from her eyes as she drew her daughter close and kissed her cheek. "I feared that you were in love with love. But now I know that you are truly in love, not with an idea, but with a man who wants only what is best for you."

"Aye. I'm so fortunate, Mum."

"Indeed."

Kylia hugged her grandmother and her sisters, before turning to accept congratulations from old Bessie and Jeremy.

Dougal was beaming as he kissed Kylia's cheek. "I now have a sister."

"And I have a brother. It is something I have long desired."

With a grin Dougal caught Grant in a fierce bear hug. "You chose well, my brother."

When the two stepped apart, Grant met his eyes and nodded. "I always choose well. Not only my wife, but my brother. For you are my brother, Dougal. If we were not born of the same mother, we were borne of the same blood. We are brothers of the heart. For now. For always."

At his words, Hazlet, who had held back, strode forward and offered her hand. "I offer you my warmest wishes, nephew. This day I have been reborn. I can now die a happy woman."

Grant took her hand and drew her close. "But can you…live a happy woman, Aunt?"

His question caught her by surprise, causing her to pull back. "What do you mean?"

"If you truly are reborn, there must be a reason for it. Perhaps you're meant to learn how to live in joy for a change, instead of living always in grief."

He saw the light of understanding in her eyes.

"I believe you're right, nephew. I mean to try." She surprised them both by stepping close to press a kiss to his cheek.

As she started to back away, he drew her close and kissed her on the cheek. "There, now, Aunt, that didn't hurt, did it? Perhaps when we return to Duncrune, you might allow Lord Giles to do the same."

She merely stared at him in stunned surprise before turning to Kylia. "There is about you, my lady, a look of serenity that is most attractive." She took her hands. Squeezed. "I hope you will teach me how to love, and forgive, and to find the peace and serenity that you've found."

Kylia smiled. "I believe you're already learning, Aunt Hazlet."

Grant took his wife's hand. "We must leave, my love, for my people..." He paused and smiled. "Our people are in need of us."

"Aye." She scooped up the wolf pup, and turned for a last look at her family, who were so dear to her.

"You'll bring our Kylia back to us often, won't you, my lord?" Nola called.

"You know I will, my lady, for I crave the

peace and beauty of your kingdom as much as she.''

As Grant and Kylia joined hands with Dougal and Hazlet, Wilona began to chant the ancient words that would take them away. Soon Nola and her daughters joined in, sending them off in a chorus of song.

With the words ringing in their ears, they began to float high over the hills and valleys, over villages and wild, forested countrysides, until far below they spotted the familiar village of Duncrune, and just beyond, the castle.

As they began their descent, Grant drew Kylia close. ''Welcome home, my love.''

Home. The word had her weeping again. But these were tears of such joy, for she was now where she belonged, with the man who had owned her heart from the beginning of her life. The man who would, she now knew, be with her until the very end of time.

* * * * *

Read youngest sister Gwenellen's story in THE KNIGHT AND THE SEER, coming in October 2003, only in Harlequin Historicals.

ITCHIN' FOR SOME ROLLICKING ROMANCES SET ON THE AMERICAN FRONTIER? THEN TAKE A GANDER AT THESE TANTALIZING TALES FROM HARLEQUIN HISTORICALS

On sale September 2003

WINTER WOMAN by Jenna Kernan
(Colorado, 1835)

After braving the winter alone in the Rockies, a defiant woman is entrusted to the care of a gruff trapper!

THE MATCHMAKER by Lisa Plumley
(Arizona territory, 1882)

Will a confirmed bachelor be bitten by the love bug when he woos a young woman in order to flush out the mysterious Morrow Creek matchmaker?

On sale October 2003

WYOMING WILDCAT by Elizabeth Lane
(Wyoming, 1866)

A blizzard ignites hot-blooded passions between a white medicine woman and an amnesiac man, but an ominous secret looms on the horizon....

THE OTHER GROOM by Lisa Bingham
(Boston and New York, 1870)

When a penniless woman masquerades as the daughter of a powerful marquis, her intended groom risks it all to protect her from harm!

Visit us at www.eHarlequin.com

HARLEQUIN HISTORICALS®

HHWEST27

Travel back in time to the British and Scottish Isles with Harlequin Historicals

On Sale July 2003

BEAUCHAMP BESIEGED by Elaine Knighton
(England, 1206-1210)

A feisty Welshwoman and a fierce English knight are used as political pawns—and discover the passion of a lifetime!

THE BETRAYAL by Ruth Langan
(Scotland, 1500s)

When a highland laird fights his way into the Mystical Kingdom to prevent a grave injustice, will he become spellbound by an enchanting witch?

On Sale August 2003

A DANGEROUS SEDUCTION
by Patricia Frances Rowell
(England, 1816)

An earl hell-bent on revenge discovers the fine line between hate and love when he falls for the wife of his mortal enemy!

A MOMENT'S MADNESS by Helen Kirkman
(England, 917 A.D.)

With danger swirling around them, will a courageous Danish woman and a fearless Saxon warrior find their heart's desire in each other's arms?

Visit us at www.eHarlequin.com

HARLEQUIN HISTORICALS®

HHMED31

eHARLEQUIN.com

Your favorite authors are just a click away
at www.eHarlequin.com!

- Take our **Sister Author Quiz** and
  we'll match you up with the author
  most like you!

- Choose from over 500
  author **profiles!**

- Chat with your favorite authors
  on our **message boards.**

- Are you an author in the making?
  Get advice from published authors
  in **The Inside Scoop!**

- Get the latest on **author appearances**
  and tours!

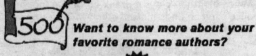

500 *Want to know more about your
favorite romance authors?*

Choose from over 500 author profiles!

**Learn about your favorite authors
in a fun, interactive setting—
visit www.eHarlequin.com today!**

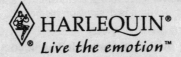

LOOKIN' FOR RIVETING TALES ABOUT RUGGED MEN AND THE FEISTY LADIES WHO TRY TO TAME THEM?

From Harlequin Historicals

July 2003

TEXAS GOLD by Carolyn Davidson

A fiercely independent farmer's past catches up with her when the husband she left behind turns up on her doorstep!

OF MEN AND ANGELS by Victoria Bylin

Can a hard-edged outlaw find redemption—and true love—in the arms of an angelic young woman?

On sale August 2003

BLACKSTONE'S BRIDE by Bronwyn Williams

Will a beleaguered gold miner's widow and a wounded half-breed ignite a searing passion when they form a united front?

HIGH PLAINS WIFE by Jillian Hart

A taciturn rancher proposes a marriage of convenience to a secretly smitten spinster who has designs on his heart!

Visit us at www.eHarlequin.com

HARLEQUIN HISTORICALS®